His Yuletide Kiss

A FIRST KISS REGENCY ROMANCE

L SUMMER HANFORD

This is a work of fiction. Names, characters, businesses, places, events, locations, and incidents are either the products of the author's imagination or used in a fictitious manner. However, various historical figures and locations used are employed as accurately as is practical.

ISBN: 978-1-7347793-4-9

IngramSpark Edition

Cover by Victoria Cooper Art

Dear Reader,

If you enjoy this book, and I hope you do, you'll find a link to my email list at the end. Sign up for free books, sneak previews, new release alerts, news, giveaways and more at:
https://geni.us/RomanceMailSignUp

Happy Reading!

MORE by SUMMER HANFORD

Historical Romance

Crown & Dagger Historical Romance
Kestrel
Red Fox
Forest Hart

First Kiss Regency Romance
His Yuletide Kiss

The Duke's Bequest
Grace's Story
Sleigh Bells & Slander
Wildflowers & Wiles
Holly & Heartache
Meadows & Mischief

Regency Romance by Summer Hanford - From Scarsdale Publishing

Songs of Rebellion Series
Ballad of Discord

Under the Shadow of the Marquess Series
The Archaeologist's Daughter*
The Duke's Widow*
The False Lady*

From Scarsdale's Marriage Maker Series
One Good Gentleman
My Lady of Danger

Rake Ruiner
Dreaming of a Gentleman
My Lady My Siren
The Runaway Baroness
His Imaginary Courtship

Ladies Always Shoot First Half Hour Reads*
Captured by a Duke
To Save a Lord
One Shot for a Gentleman
Anything for a Lord

A Lord's Kiss Half Hour Reads*
Last Chance for a Lord
To Know a Lord's Kiss
A Lord's Dream
Deceived by a Lord

Children's Picture Books

Boxing Day
Lufu
Bunny Lore

Pride and Prejudice Retellings by Renata McMann and Summer Hanford

To Fall for Mr. Darcy
Mr. Collins' Will
After Anne
More Than He Seems
Their Secret Love
A Duel in Meryton*
Love, Letters and Lies
The Long Road to Longbourn
Hypothetically Married*
The Forgiving Season
The Widow Elizabeth
Foiled Elopement
Believing in Darcy
Her Final Wish
Miss Bingley's Christmas
Epiphany with Tea
Courting Elizabeth
The Fire at Netherfield Park
From Ashes to Heiresses*
Entanglements of Honor
Lady Catherine Regrets
A Death at Rosings
Mary Younge
Poor Mr. Darcy
Mr. Collins' Deception
The Scandalous Stepmother
Caroline and the Footman
Elizabeth's Plight (The Wickham Coin Book II)
Georgiana's Folly (The Wickham Coin Book I)
The Second Mrs. Darcy

His Yuletide Kiss

Chapter One

Seated on the opposite end of the sofa, Arthur watched, mesmerized, as Wendy Barlow fluttered a fan before her lips. The red-dyed bow of her mouth was there, and then not. There, and then not. She loved to taunt him with what he wanted but couldn't yet have.

Little did she know, in preparation for her twenty-first birthday, only six weeks away, he'd written to his uncle with word that he intended to ask for her hand. Not only because courtesy dictated he inform the man who'd raised him, but also because advance knowledge of any plan to propose was a stipulation of his uncle's patronage. Not that Uncle Garrick had much choice on where to bestow his favor, or his fortune. Arthur, and his younger sister Lillian, were Uncle Garrick's only relations.

Above the fluttering fan, Wendy's blue eyes gleamed. She knew the effect her teasing had, the spell she wove about him. Arthur minded not at all. He and Wendy Barlow were fated for one another. Arthur simply awaited his uncle's return letter and then he would make his courtship official.

Several years ago, when Arthur first met Wendy's twin, Wendel, at university, they'd sparked an immediate friendship. Despite his kinship with Wendel, Arthur had never dreamed that taking his Yuletide break at the Barlows' country manor would acquaint him with the woman with whom he would spend the remainder of his days. Since that fateful winter, Arthur had become nearly a resident of Barlow Manor, content under Wendy's spell.

She continued to flutter her fan, decorated with a scene of Dolus sculpting Mendacium, which happened to be her favorite of Aesop's Fables. Arthur appreciated the effort Wendy put into her flirtation, especially since the mid-March weather boasted no warmth. In fact, across the room where Wendel sat at a solitary game of cards, a fire danced between two marble pillars below an unmodish, ostentatiously ornate mantle.

Seeing Wendel fully engrossed in his game, Arthur stretched an arm out along the back of the sofa. Perhaps he would cast off propriety for once and wind a single curl about his index finger. He adored Wendy's silken tresses. White-gold like sunshine sparkling off water. So unlike the harshly black locks that marked his own family. Gaze locked with his, she lowered her fan. His daring grew. He reached out. He halted the motion, his hand a hairsbreadth from her smooth skin. To touch her when he'd not even announced a courtship would be an affront to society and disrespectful of her.

An ache filled him. They'd waited a long time to declare their intentions. Arthur would have pressed for a wedding ages ago, but her father had been ill since before Arthur met her, and had died a little over a year past. The time had never been right to ask for Wendy's hand. Now, not only was her year of mourning finished, Arthur had attained his majority and, in a month, she would achieve hers. Only hearing from his uncle held them back.

He needed Uncle Garrick's blessing to remain in the old man's graces. Arthur's parents had left him and his sister with almost nothing. It was Uncle Garrick's fortune that Arthur would someday inherit, and it was by their uncle's whim that they afforded their gentrified existence. That being the case, Arthur's letter had also hinted at a raise in his allowance, to better support Wendy.

"I don't recall hearing any banns read," Wendel said in a mild tone.

Startled, Arthur jerked his hand back and cast his friend a sheepish look. He hadn't noticed Wendel look up from his game. Wendy's mien expressed chagrin, but Arthur felt only relief that he hadn't overstepped and actually touched her.

Wendy's fan flipped back up. "Don't be tiresome, Wendel."

"I'm your brother. If I don't defend your honor, who will?"

"I can defend my own honor."

The twins glared at one another, wearing matching frowns.

"You know my intentions are honorable," Arthur inserted. "And I didn't lay a finger on Miss Barlow. There is no reason for agitation."

Wendy turned her frown his way. "Your intentions and the placement of your fingers matter not in the slightest. I am perfectly capable of deciding if I wish to permit a man liberties with my person. It is none of Wendel's concern."

"The devil it isn't," Wendel protested. "Arthur, you have a sister. What would you do if you caught me caressing her?"

"Miss Garrick is Mr. Garrick's younger sister and his ward," Wendy said, saving Arthur from an answer which could only support Wendel's cause. "I am your older sister."

"By a quarter of an hour."

Arthur angled his head to rest on the back of the sofa and studied the ceiling, decorated with bluebirds and white clouds. Once the twins began an argument, it lasted for hours.

"It's irrelevant by how long," Wendy said primly.

"What's irrelevant is that you're older. If you were a man, it would matter, but you're only a girl, so no one cares."

Wendy's fan snapped closed. "If I were a man, I would march over there and—"

"Children, I have news," Mrs. Barlow said, gliding into the room, feet making no sound despite the thinness of the threadbare carpet.

Arthur stood to bow, using the movement to hide his smile. As Wendy's voice, especially, was quite piercing, Mrs. Barlow had surely heard, and elected to ignore, the ongoing argument. Propriety seen to, Arthur retook his seat to attend to Mrs. Barlow's news.

She halted in the middle of the room, blocking

the twins from glaring at each other, and said, "Your cousin, Daphne, is coming to visit."

Arthur cast a quick glance at Wendy. She and Wendel rarely mentioned their cousins, the Hayhursts, and then only disparagingly. Arthur knew little of them, as they hadn't ventured from their country seat in over twenty years. They did possess a townhome on one of the fanciest streets in London, but always let it out, requiring the funds.

"Cousin Daphne? Here?" Wendy's gaze narrowed. "When?"

"You should have consulted us, Mother," Wendel added.

"We don't wish to have any Hayhursts here, Mother," Wendy said sternly.

"I did not ask what you wish, dear." Mrs. Barlow's tone held unflappable calm. "Nor was there any need for me to consult either of you."

Wendel puffed out his chest, his least endearing habit. "Father left everything to me, including this manor. You need not consult Wendy, but you should have discussed inviting our cousin with me."

Mrs. Barlow turned her mild expression on her son. "Yes, your father did leave everything to you, Wendel, and I am sure that you'll find taking over management from me enlightening, but until your twenty-first birthday, manage I will, in my capacity as your guardian. As such, I invited your cousin Daphne to visit for the month of April."

Frowning, Wendel drummed his fingers on the

card table. "I see. You deliberately sneaked this visit in before our birthday."

"Sneaked is an unpleasant word, Wendel," Mrs. Barlow said with a touch of sternness. "Besides which, your aunt already wrote back, accepting."

Wendy made a tsking sound. "For certain Aunt Hayhurst accepted. They're happy to foist a daughter off on us. They've seven children to settle, four of them girls." She looked around her mother to her brother. "Beware, Wendel, Cousin Daphne is likely coming here to ensnare you."

Wendel slapped his palm flat on the table, displacing his cards. "She'd best not be. I won't give charity where Father did not deign to."

"Oh Wendel," Mrs. Barlow said sadly. "If only I could count on you not to do things your father did do, rather than the ones he did not."

Arthur's eyebrows shot up. Would he finally hear why Mrs. Barlow and Mr. Barlow had never got on? He'd heard rumors, to be sure, but knew better than to count rumor as truth. The source of the rift between the twins' parents was the greatest secret of the household, and the one secret the twins would never impart.

Wendy let out an exaggerated sigh. "You are so tedious, Mother."

"Mother, Father's poor behavior regarding you was a lifetime ago," Wendel said, his tone kinder.

"Oh? How long ago, then, did the divide between your father and Mr. Hayhurst form?" Smugness lurked around the edges of Mrs. Barlow's tone. "It seems to me that if one transgression should be forgiven on the basis of time, so should the other."

"Except that Father was innocent of the charges Uncle Hayhurst made against him," Wendy snapped.

Mrs. Barlow shrugged, usual calmness firmly back in place. "That is a matter of opinion."

"Father assured us of his innocence," Wendel stated.

Wendy held up a staying hand. "Let us not have this discussion again, especially in front of our guest."

Wendel leaned to the side to look past his mother to his sister. "Garrick is practically family."

Wendy, too, adjusted her pose, to better glare at her brother. "We are not discussing the matter." Her voice held a hard edge.

Mrs. Barlow stepped between them again. "Regardless, I have invited Daphne for the month of April. She will celebrate your birthday with us. It is a good opportunity to come to know your cousin a bit before the Season begins. Daphne and Christine will come out together this autumn, so we are certain to encounter them all in London."

Wendel let out a groan. "They'll be a constant bother, our poor relations trying to use our connections to get ahead."

"Isn't Cousin Christine rather young to come out?" Wendy asked. "I suppose they plan to save money by combining the girls' Seasons, which also explains why they've let Cousin Daphne get so old before giving her one."

"Christine has seventeen years and Daphne twenty," Mrs. Barlow said. "Both perfectly respectable ages at which to have a come out. May I remind you, Wendy, that you will be one and twenty when you come out this autumn."

"Yes, but because of Father's illness and passing. Not because we're poor."

Mrs. Barlow let out a long, slow sigh. "You are ever your father's daughter."

Wendy tipped her chin in the air. "Of course."

Arthur couldn't help but admire her regal bearing. A man would win envy with such a stately woman on his arm.

"Regardless, when your cousin arrives, try to find it in your heart to be civil." Mrs. Barlow shifted to include Wendel in her stern look. "You as well. Now that your father is gone, I intend to have my sister back."

Arthur worked not to let his interest register on his face. So it was true that the alienation between Mr. and Mrs. Barlow had something to do with Mrs. Barlow's sister, Mrs. Hayhurst. Maybe the rumors he'd heard, regarding the two gentlemen and an actress, were indeed true.

"Now, if you will excuse me, I have preparations to make." Mrs. Barlow angled a pleasant expression at Arthur. "And a good day to you, Mr. Garrick," she added, then turned and strode from the room.

Arthur rose quickly to bow at her retreating back. As her footsteps faded down the hall, he settled back onto the edge of the sofa. He adjusted his place, seeking comfort on a cushion in need of new stuffing, and looked from one twin to the other.

"Come, you must tell me at last. Why did your father and Mr. Hayhurst dislike one another so, and what does it have to do with your mother and father always being at odds?"

Wendy's full lips formed into a pout. She crossed her arms over her chest, mien mulish.

Arthur wished he were at liberty to kiss that expression away.

Wendel rolled his shoulders. "Well, if Cousin Daphne is coming here, maybe it's time you know."

"Wendel," Wendy gasped. "Mr. Garrick does not need to know our family's scandal."

Wendel frowned, looking from Wendy to Arthur and back again.

Arthur leaned back, adopting an indolent pose. "It's not as if I don't know. All of London whispers about how Mr. Hayhurst challenged your father over an actress. As everyone knows I am your frequent guest, I've been subjected to the rumors on more than one occasion."

Wendel shrugged. "Well then, you know the heart of it."

Arthur shook his head. "But I do not. Why would Mr. Hayhurst challenge his brother by marriage to a duel over an actress, and why would that make your mother forever angry with your father, even after his death?"

"It was all jealousy," Wendy stated. "Mr.

Hayhurst realized he'd picked the lesser sister, so he invented an affair between Father and some actress, and then he challenged Father in order to create a scandal."

"Hayhurst was also jealous of our father's wealth," Wendel added.

Arthur schooled his expression. Wendel and Wendy always spoke as if their father had possessed a great fortune, but Arthur had heard more rumors than simply those about the actress. He wouldn't quite call the Barlows poor, but certainly not wealthy. Gossip bandied about London said that the twins' father had invested foolishly and gambled heavily before he became ill. After, he'd spent liberally on any purported cure, though all knew one couldn't cure the pox.

"So," Arthur drawled, trying to draw out the truth. "Your Uncle Hayhurst wanted to marry your mother, but your father won her. In retribution, your uncle created an imaginary affair, then challenged your father to ensure that all of London heard the rumor?"

Wendel nodded. "Exactly."

"But, wouldn't that cause a rift between your mother and her sister as well, and not between your mother and father?"

Wendy shook her head, firelight gilding her curls. "Mother, foolishly, believed the rumor."

"And she remains angry with your father even now? For bedding an actress over twenty years ago?" Arthur understood that women didn't enjoy having their menfolk dally with others, but to hold one indiscretion against your husband for all time? Even on his deathbed?

Wendy gave him a stern look. "We Barlow women do not take kindly to being betrayed, Mr. Garrick."

Wendel chuckled. "Consider yourself warned, Garrick."

Arthur turned on the sofa to fully meet Wendy's eyes. "I would never betray you, Miss Barlow."

She rewarded his declaration with a sweet smile.

Wendel groaned. "Ug. All you two have done this morning is make calf eyes at each other. Come, play cards with me, both of you, or I will entice Arthur away to practice fencing."

Wendy stood, causing both gentlemen to rise. "Go and fence," she said. "I must inventory my jewelry and decide what to lock away while Cousin Daphne is here. If the father is a liar, there's no reason to think the daughter won't steal."

Though Arthur thought that a bit extreme, he nodded, then locked an admiring gaze on Wendy as she swept from the room. Once she disappeared from sight, he turned to Wendel, who eyed him with amusement. Arthur cleared his throat, feeling a touch guilty for ogling his closest friend's sister. "Best out of five?"

Wendel nodded, standing. "Aye, and be forewarned, I intend to take you to task for the way you look at my sister."

"You'll attempt to take me to task, you mean, and she'll be my bride soon enough." With that thought to buoy him, Arthur led the way from the parlor, intent on proving his righteousness on Wendel's person.

Chapter Two

Daphne sat on her favorite floral sofa, carefully altering the neckline of one of her mother's gowns. Pale yellow like the roses in the rose-and-vine pattern on the sofa, the gown was a favorite. Daphne held fond memories of her mother wearing the dress for one of their family's annual Yuletide balls, spied on through the railing. More lovely than Daphne could ever hope to be, Mother had cut an elegant figure on the dance floor with Father. Her mother hadn't donned the gown in the years following, but Daphne had aspired to wear it ever since that magical night well over a decade ago.

"You know, Daphne dear, you, Christine and I could take our fashion hunting trip to London earlier than planned," Mother said from where she sat reading on the opposite sofa, one upholstered in white with yellow and green stripes. "We still have time to commission new gowns for your trip to the Barlows."

Where she played chess with the eldest of their brothers, Christine raised hazel eyes from the board. "I don't need a new wardrobe," she said and moved a pawn.

Opposite her, their brother Edward slid his knight across the board, a move Christine instantly countered.

"Nor do I require a new wardrobe at this time,

but thank you, Mother." Daphne fished more thread from her sewing basket. "My cousins are hardly out of mourning. They're likely still in grays. I don't wish to appear too showy by comparison."

Her father, seated in a green armchair by one of the tall windows that opened onto the back lawn, shook his paper, but declined to lower it and contribute. Through the open window, the laughter of the younger two Hayhurst boys rang out, followed by the angry squeals of the youngest two girls. No one in the parlor evidenced concern, aware that their nanny oversaw them.

"I don't understand why Daphne must go to the Barlows at all." Christine's tone held a note of aggrievement. "This is our last spring all together."

"We won't all be together," Edward said as he pushed his bishop across the board. "I am going to stay with a school chum."

"No one cares where you're going to be, Edward," Christine said as she moved another of the small ivory figures.

Edward made a countermove, saying, "Everyone cares. Besides which, there's no way to know this is our last summer all together."

Christine thumped a chess piece down onto the board. "Of course it is. We're having a Season. Daphne is sure to find a husband with alacrity, and I will wed Ryan, and we will go off to homes of our own."

"You aren't to call him by his Christian name," Edward said. A glance showed his expression to be as unforgiving as his tone. He snatched up a pawn and slapped it down a square away. "We're all grown now. You must call him Mr. Quincy."

"You call him Ryan," Christine replied.

"I'm not a girl."

"I'm not a girl either. I'm a lady."

"You're a girl. I can tell by how you play chess."

Christine moved her queen. "You mean, the way I'm beating you at chess?"

"Children," Mother said in a longsuffering tone.

"He began it," Christine said in the same breath as Edward said, "She started it."

"And I am finishing it." Mother's clipped words brooked no further argument.

Daphne hid a smile and concentrated on her stitches.

"Daphne is going to the Barlows because we're certain to encounter them in town this autumn," Mother continued into the now-silent room. "As your father no longer holds a disagreement with Mr. Barlow senior, we will be polite and socialize with your aunt and cousins. Daphne is the foundation layer for a cheerful Season in their company."

"She's more like the sacrificial lamb," Edward muttered.

"Are you ever going to move, Edward?" Christine demanded. "I will get the hourglass if you can't keep a decent pace."

Daphne glanced up to see a frown touch her mother's harried countenance.

"Furthermore, Edward is correct, Christine," Mother continued. "You are not to refer to Mr. Quincy by his Christian name, or to speak of him as your betrothed. Your father hasn't given him permission to court you, let alone for the two of you to wed."

"Only because Father is being obstinate."

Across the parlor, Father rattled his paper again.

Christine tossed golden curls that Daphne couldn't help but envy, and eyed the rattling paper, saying, "Well, you are, Papa."

Daphne looked across the room to beg silence from her younger sister with her gaze, but Christine glared at the paper held before their father. Must they all endure Christine's rant yet again? It was obvious to everyone, except apparently her sister, that Father did not intend to change his mind.

"It's your move again," Edward said.

"I know you're listening, Father," Christine snapped. She drew in a deep breath. "You aren't being fair," she continued in a more pleading tone.

Father lowered his paper, revealing a swath of brown, gray-streaked hair. Amber eyes, mirrored in Daphne's face, regarded Christine patiently. "Someday, you will realize that I am being fair. What wouldn't be fair to you is to permit you to wed the first man you ever noticed, without permitting you the chance to meet others. Especially when the bulk of your dowry would go immediately to pay his debts."

Christine folded her arms across her chest. "When I was fourteen, you said I was too young to marry Ryan before he went away to fight on the Continent. When his older brother died and he came back, I was sixteen, so not too young anymore, but you said I couldn't marry him until he paid off the debt his brother had amassed while managing the estate. Well, he's running the estate at a profit and paying down the debt. When will you be satisfied?"

Father shook his head. "When he has paid every last penny without the benefit of your dowry. The money I've settled on you is meant to ensure that you and your children have a good life, not to repair the damage done by Mr. Quincy's miscreant older brother." Father eyed Christine sternly. "Besides which, you must live life a bit before making such a momentous decision. One Season. That is all I ask. See what other gentlemen England has to offer. Then, if you still love Mr. Quincy, he may court you and, once his debts are paid, he may wed you."

"He'll be ten years paying off the collectors, Chris, so you may as well have a Season," Edward added. "Father is right. Until he pays it all off, you'll never know Quincy isn't simply after your dowry."

Daphne set down her needle and covered her ears.

"How dare you?" Christine shrieked. "Ryan loves me. He would marry me even without a dowry."

"Then let father offer him your hand without one and see what he says."

"You just want more money for yourself."

Hands still clamped over her ears, Daphne glanced at the chandelier in the center of the room, sure that the volume of her sister's voice made the crystals vibrate.

Edward half stood to lean across the table. "I do n—"

"Children," Mother and Father said simultaneously.

Father stood. He dropped the paper, open to an article about shipping, onto a nearby table. "Edward, come with me."

Daphne lowered her hands from her ears. She didn't need to follow and listen to know which lecture Edward would get. It would be the one about how, even though he was the eldest son and a man of nineteen, he was not his sisters' keeper. Father would continue to watch over them, as he always had, as would their mother. They did not require a third parent.

"But she hasn't moved yet," Edward muttered, tone sullen, as he straightened to stand.

"Here." Christine snapped a piece down on the chessboard. "Check mate."

Edward's mulish expression morphed into a scowl.

"Edward, with me," Father reiterated and crossed to the parlor door.

Face angled to the plush floral carpet, Edward shuffled off after their father.

Outside, another bout of laughter and squeals sounded. Daphne could guess that interaction as well. Her younger two brothers, aged fourteen and thirteen, were tormenting her youngest sisters, who were eleven and eight and loved to stage elaborate parties for their dolls. Like as not, dolls were being carried up trees and held hostage in exchange for whatever treats the girls had finagled from their cook. Their nanny would ignore the spectacle unless one of the boys climbed too high or demanded too steep a payment.

"You are not to speak to your father that way, Christine," Mother said in a soft voice.

Christine began resetting the chess pieces.

"I mean it," Mother said.

Pink rose in Christine's cheeks. Daphne wondered if she ought to cover her ears again, but her sister looked up with wide hazel eyes. Tentatively, Daphne poked the needle she held through the fabric of the gown.

"Why doesn't he wish me to wed Mr. Quincy? I've loved him since I was a girl. For how many years must I be consistent before Father admits my heart will not be changed?"

"Your father doesn't wish for you to be too hasty. You have your whole life to be wed, once the choice is made."

Christine shook her head, curls bouncing. "You and Father are still in love. Anyone can see that. How can a man who loves his wife as he does not believe in the love I bear for Ry—For Mr. Quincy?"

Mother let out a sigh. "I know you believe, having seen seventeen years, that you know the world, but you will have to accept that your father has lived more than twice as long and knows more than twice as much."

Christine folded her arms across her chest. "I do not have to accept that. I—"

"Christine," Mother interrupted.

"What?"

"Go to your room, dear. Spend some time in quiet contemplation. Come out when you feel you can use a civil tone and show deference to your elders."

Christine surged to her feet. "Fine." She stamped from the room.

Daphne once more dropped her needle and put her hands over her ears. The parlor door slammed shut behind her sister. This time, there could be no doubt that the crystals of the chandelier shook, giving off a tinkling sound as they collided.

Mother let out another sigh, closed her book, and scrubbed both hands over her face. Daphne resumed her work on the gown.

Without the excessive hoops that had been popular when her mother first wore the dress, the hem required taking up. Daphne had already adjusted the waistline and added lace to the bodice, for a touch more modesty.

"Daphne," Mother said.

Daphne lifted her gaze. "Yes?"

"Do you feel that Christine's attachment to Mr. Quincy is genuine?"

Daphne pressed her lips together, thinking, then offered, "It's difficult to say. Knowing Christine, she could very well convince herself of unflagging affection out of stubbornness." Daphne conjured an image of Mr. Quincy. Wavy brown hair. Earnest blue eyes. The puppy-dog look he always aimed at Christine, even after fighting on the front and returning home to manage an estate driven into debt by his older brother. "I believe Mr. Quincy to be genuinely attached to her."

"Well, that is something, at least." Mother drummed her fingers on the closed volume in her lap, her expression thoughtful.

"Mother?" Daphne asked tentatively, emboldened by her mother seeking her opinion concerning Christine.

Her mother's bright blue eyes focused on her. "Yes, dear?"

"If I'm going to Aunt Barlow's to lay the foundation for familial comradery, may I know the cause of Father and Uncle Barlow's feud?"

Daphne had expected another sigh, but her mother studied her calmly. Daphne held her breath, unsure how to sway her mother's assessment. She and Edward had devoted many a whispered conversation to speculation on the nature of their father and Uncle Barlow's dispute.

Mother dropped her gaze. "I suppose you should. Your cousins will undoubtedly have a version, and when we go to London this autumn, others will as well."

"People in London know?"

Daphne's parents never went to London. They had a townhome there, but had always rented it out, until this spring. Now, it underwent renovations to ready for their arrival later in the year.

Mother nodded. "Yes, everyone in London knows. At least, any who care to. It's common knowledge." She grimaced. "At the heart of it, your father and uncle clashed over a woman. An actress." Mother said the word with distaste. "Your father challenged your uncle for her affection. Your uncle refused to fight and was branded a coward."

"That's all?" Daphne asked when her mother offered no additional information.

Mother nodded.

"That has kept our families apart for over twenty years?"

Mother shrugged. "It's a bit more complicated than that, I suppose, and it didn't help that Mr. Barlow forbade your aunt to receive letters from me or to write to me."

"Father didn't enjoin you similarly?"

"Your father realized that the entire incident was farcical and apologized to me. I cannot know for certain, but I don't believe my sister received a similar apology. It's my understanding, from the few letters we've exchanged since your uncle's death, that my sister never forgave her husband and they never reconciled."

Daphne narrowed her gaze. "Why would Father and Uncle Barlow need to apologize to you and Aunt Barlow?"

Mother made a swishing gesture with her hand. "That is all in the past, dear, and should remain there. All you need to know is that your father and

I love each other and were both saddened not to see your aunt for so many years, or to know your cousins as they grew." With that, Mother dropped her gaze and opened her book.

Daphne frowned but took back up her needle. As she sewed, she endeavored to guess what her mother hadn't said. The occasional glance at her mother's set expression, maintained even as she read, revealed that no more information would be forthcoming.

Daphne finished the hem and began packing away her needle, thimble and thread. That accomplished, she carefully folded the made over gown, intending to try it on that evening. Footsteps, muted by the closed parlor door, sounded without. The door opened to reveal her father.

"Good day, dear," Father said, offering Mother a smile, which she readily returned. He then shifted his attention to Daphne. "Daphne, a word in the library?"

"Yes, Father."

Leaving her sewing on the sofa, Daphne rose. She hadn't misbehaved like Edward and Christine. Did her father, like her mother, plan a confession? She hoped as much as she crossed the room, feeling her mother's gaze on her.

Chapter Three

Arthur reined in his mount at the top of a hill overlooking the Barlows' manor, taking in the large glossy carriage leaving the front entrance. Pulled by a perfectly matched foursome of Friesians and manned by a coachman and two tigers, all in livery, the thickly lacquered conveyance was one of the finest he'd ever seen. As he surveyed the scene below, two of the Barlows' footmen appeared in the courtyard to hoist a large trunk from the drive and carry it around to the back of the manor.

Wendel caught up and brought his mount to a halt beside Arthur, releasing a low whistle. "Who owns that beauty?"

"What beauty?" Wendy's tone held annoyance.

When they raced, she preferred the gentlemen to permit her to win. Arthur normally did, but his stallion had wished to run and he'd already endured an entire month of Wendel claiming to be the superior rider. In this fresh month of April, Arthur intended for Wendel to know a change of fortune in that respect.

"That carriage." Wendel pointed to where the conveyance rumbled away down the road.

"It's gorgeous." Wendy turned bright eyes on Arthur. "Is it your uncle's? Do you suppose he will give it to you along with the rest of his holdings?"

Arthur shook his head. "It's not Uncle Garrick's. Isn't your cousin to arrive today? Perhaps it's the Hayhursts'?"

Wendy sniffed. "How could they afford such a magnificent carriage?"

Arthur had no ready reply. People who hadn't been able to reside in London for over twenty years, who planned to combine Seasons for their twenty-year-old and seventeen-year-old daughters, couldn't afford a carriage like the one that crested a hill and disappeared from sight before them.

"We won't find out from here," Wendel said. "Race you to the stable." He prodded his mount with his heels and the beast leaped forward down the hill.

"Cheater," Arthur called and plunged after.

Distantly, he heard Wendy's shout of annoyance, but kept his focus on navigating the hillside down which he and Wendel careened. In short order, he passed his friend. Arthur hit the valley floor and angled for the stable, Wendel falling farther behind.

Arthur reached the stable and pulled to a halt. He leaped from the saddle as a groom came forward to take his mount. "Be sure to walk him until he is cool, and treat him well. He won two races today."

"Yes, sir," the groom said, then walked the stallion away.

Wendel clattered up to the stable door. "I thought I had you that time, Garrick."

Arthur grinned. "You'll have to cheat better if

you want to best me."

Wendel swung a leg over the saddle and dropped to the ground. "Next time, I will."

A second groom led Wendel's gelding away and they both turned to wait while Wendy wound down the hillside. She had an admirable seat, back straight and expression poised. The very vision of a genteel lady. Arthur couldn't help a swell of pride that she'd soon be his.

"She's taking forever," Wendel muttered. He cupped his hands around his mouth and shouted, "Oy, Wendy, get a move on."

Arthur rubbed at the light stubble on his chin, hiding his amusement as Wendy's head swiveled to reveal her scowl.

Wendel took a half step backward. "Oh, she's angry now."

"We did leave her behind twice."

"Well, I'm going to leave her behind again. I don't need a pre-dinner tongue lashing." Wendel turned a narrowed gaze on Arthur. "I expect my sister to reach the house unmussed."

Arthur held out his hands, palms forward to ward off Wendel's mistrust. "If Miss Barlow is mussed in any way, it's from her ride."

Wendel snorted. "Wendy doesn't ride fast enough to get wind tousled."

"Then I imagine she will arrive at the house a vision of perfection."

Wendel darted a look up the roadway leading to the stable, along which Wendy marched her mare. "And I will arrive at the house unchastised." He flashed a grin and set off at a jog.

"Wendel Barlow, don't you dare run off," Wendy screeched.

Wendel waved but didn't turn back as he pelted for the house.

Wendy drew her mount to a halt alongside Arthur and looked down her nose at him. "And what do you have to say for yourself, Mr. Garrick?"

"That you are lovely when your eyes flash with anger, Miss Barlow."

She tipped her head to the side, considering his words. Finally, she nodded. "You may help me down, Mr. Garrick."

Aware that several grooms loitered in the stable entrance, Arthur carefully clasped Wendy's slim waist and lifted her down. The moment he set her on her feet, he dropped his arms and stepped back, which earned him an eye roll. One of the grooms came forward to collect her mount.

"That was hardly the… assistance for which I'd hoped," she said.

"That was the assistance of a gentleman," he countered, then offered his arm. "May I escort you to the house?"

"You may." Wendy placed her hand lightly on his arm. "Let us take the garden path."

Arthur frowned, for that was the least direct path, but dutifully directed his steps in that direction. Wendy took up a diatribe about Wendel's behavior as they walked. Arthur tried to focus on the scenery, rather than her words.

The Barlows' garden was sizable, but poorly

tended. What might once have been beguiling topiaries were now little more than confusing, shaggy blobs. The grass always stood too high. Weeds crept between large flat rocks and dotted gravel pathways much in need of a fresh coat of stone. One of the fountains they passed no longer ran, and another gurgled fitfully, the mouth of the urn the Grecian-clad young woman poured from clogged with algae. In the beds, flowers mingled indiscriminately with wild plants.

Still, the swath of clouds above was painted shades of orange and pink by the lowering sun and the late afternoon air was mild, especially for April. Wendy fell silent as they stepped into the gazebo at the center of the garden, a six-sided structure through which all the paths crossed. Arthur made to take the path that would lead from the gazebo to the manor, but she dropped his arm.

He turned back to find her looking up at him through lowered lashes.

"Kiss me," she breathed.

Arthur took a half step back, startled. "Here? Now?"

He'd longed to taste Wendy's lips, dreamed of doing so for years, but he'd made assurances to Wendel, and her brother was correct, they were not wed. Not even promised or officially courting.

"Yes. Here. Now." She fluttered her lashes and leaned closer to him.

Arthur took another step back. "It wouldn't be right."

Her expression morphed from coy to

censorious. "Last month, you nearly touched my cheek. I thought that meant something, Arthur. I thought the time was near for us to become better acquainted."

"It is. We will. I wrote to my uncle."

She leaned forward, her expression eager. "And?"

"Well… he hasn't yet replied."

She flung up her hands. "My birthday fast approaches and he hasn't yet replied? What will you do if he does not?"

Arthur squared his shoulders. "Ask for your hand, of course. If he hasn't answered by your birthday, he has no right to offer his opinion. I am a man grown, after all. I informed him of my intention to propose only as a courtesy." He grimaced. "Well, and to request an increase in my allowance, as we will be two."

"Well then, if you intend to propose with or without his blessing, there's no reason not to kiss me."

Arthur swallowed. "There is every reason. I respect you too much to compromise you." His sweeping gesture encompassed her head to toe. "You are a vision of perfection, Wendy. I would not spoil that."

Her lips pursed in a pout, but she nodded. "I am rather perfect."

Arthur smiled. "You are." He offered his arm. "Now, may I escort you to the house to change for dinner, Miss Barlow?"

"You may, Mr. Garrick."

Relief filled him when she placed her hand on his arm and permitted him to direct their steps in the direction of the house once more. Wendy could be tenacious in her fits of anger. He'd no wish to spoil dinner by putting her in one of her tempers.

She turned the conversation to her and Wendel's upcoming celebration as they traversed a slightly better maintained path. Much as with her earlier rail against her brother, she required no response from Arthur to maintain her one-sided dialogue. By the time they reached the manor house steps, the sun gleamed red from behind a distant line of trees.

Arthur escorted her through the door, opened by the Barlows' butler, and bowed over her hand. "Until dinner, Miss Barlow."

She offered a dimpled smile. "Until dinner, Mr. Garrick."

Arthur stood back to watch her glide up the staircase, waited a long moment to ensure that he wouldn't meet her in the upper hall, and then followed. He entered his chambers to find his valet, Stenson, brushing his dinner jacket, his other clothing laid out and a basin of steaming water waiting.

Stenson looked up from his work as Arthur swung the door closed. "I thought your navy jacket, sir, as Miss Hayhurst has arrived."

Arthur frowned. The navy jacket was his finest. "You don't think that's a bit much for dinner with a cousin?" And wouldn't Wendy disapprove of him dressing up for Miss Hayhurst? "Have you learned aught about the young woman?"

Stenson returned to brushing. "She seems a pleasant young woman," he said, tone bland. "Delicate of features."

Arthur chuckled as he crossed to the basin. "Pretty, is she?"

"Rather."

All the more reason not to give Wendy the impression he'd put extra care into his appearance. "I'll wear the green jacket, Stenson." Arthur tugged at the knot of his cravat.

Behind him, the brushing stilled. "The green jacket, sir?"

The coat, devoid of nearly all adornment, was Arthur's favorite. Comfortable and a deep green color he felt set off his black hair and gray eyes to their best advantage, the jacket was also his oldest. While Stenson ensured that the article showed no visible wear, a lack of stylishness and general worn quality marked the coat.

"Yes, the green jacket."

It bothered Arthur not at all that Wendy's opinion of the jacket aligned with Stenson's. If anything, that should please her, Arthur wearing such a shabby coat to meet her cousin. This way, there could be no conjecture that Arthur worked to impress Miss Hayhurst.

"Very well, sir," Stenson said in his most disapproving tone.

Arthur allowed a slight smile and continued to undress.

"Do you prefer the buttercream or the marigold,

sir?"

A glance showed Stenson held two waistcoats. Again, Arthur preferred the less ostentatious choice. This was a country dinner, after all, not the London opera. "The yellow one."

"They are both shades of yellow, sir."

"No. One is orange. I'll wear the yellow one."

"Certainly, sir."

With Stenson disapproving nearly every step of the way, Arthur washed up and dressed for dinner. The end result was unassuming. Almost too casual for the evening meal. Precisely Arthur's goal.

After assessing his appearance in the mirror, Arthur turned to his valet. "Chin up, Stenson. You never know, I may spill something on the coat and ruin it."

"One can only hope, sir."

Arthur flashed a grin and stepped into the hall.

Eyes the color of dark honey met his gaze, bright under a coif of caramel ringlets. A pale-yellow gown swept downward from an elegant neck and collarbones and outlined a tall, slim form. Obviously made over, the dress was very plain, almost severe, and eminently modest. She stepped forward, even that slight movement down the length of hallway that separated them exuding grace, and essayed a tentative smile.

"Cousin?" If her eyes were dark honey, her voice was a sweet, light version of that same confection.

A chuckle sounded from Arthur's left. Wendel stepped into the hall. "I doubt anyone has ever confused us before, Garrick."

Arthur tore his gaze from the vision in the hall to nod to Wendel. "Indeed."

The young woman glided down the hall to them, bow shaped lips turned up at the corners. "I should have noted the lack of resemblance with Aunt Barlow, but I couldn't imagine who else would be in the hall."

Wendel offered a practiced bow. "I assume you are my cousin, Miss Hayhurst?"

She returned an elegant curtsy. "Daphne, please. We need not stand on formality, Cousin."

"And you must call me Wendel." Wendel bowed again.

A surge of annoyance shot through Arthur. Why did he stand mute and ignored? Clearing his throat, he took a half step forward.

"You two look as if you arrived from the last century together," Wendel said with a chuckle, gesturing from Miss Hayhurst's gown to Arthur's waistcoat, which matched the color of the dress to perfection. Wendel turned to Miss Hayhurst. "Daphne, this is my long-time friend, Mr. Garrick. Garrick, as you've likely deduced, this is Cousin Daphne."

Garrick wrenched his gaze away from those amber eyes to bow. "Miss Hayhurst."

She dipped a curtsy. "Mr. Garrick."

Wendel proffered his arm. "May I escort you to the parlor, Cousin?"

"Should we not wait for your sister?"

Wendel shook his head, arm still extended.

"Wendy prefers to be at least half an hour late. That way, everyone can watch her enter the room."

"Oh." Miss Hayhurst's tentative tone matched her movements as she placed her hand on Wendel's sleeve. "Then yes, please. I've already forgotten where your mother directed me to go."

"Right this way." Wendel turned her but looked back over his shoulder at Arthur as they started down the hall. "Come along, Garrick. No lingering in the hall waiting for Wendy." To Miss Hayhurst he added, in a stage whisper louder than his usual speaking voice, "Garrick and Wendy are just shy of declaring an understanding, so I'm obligated to keep an eye on him."

"Oh." Miss Hayhurst sounded surprised this time. She cast a quick look over her shoulder as well, showing off that elegant neck.

Feeling decidedly out of sorts, Arthur followed Wendel and Miss Hayhurst through the manor. When they reached the parlor where the family routinely met before supper, Mrs. Barlow waited for them. She rose and crossed to take both of Miss Hayhurst's hands.

"Daphne, dear, it's lovely to have you in our home." Mrs. Barlow looked her niece up and down. "You do so resemble your father."

Arthur supposed that explained why she didn't look much like Mrs. Barlow, or Wendel and Wendy, all of whom were blonde haired and blue eyed. Both Barlow women stood of a height with Miss Hayhurst but boasted more curves to capture a man's interest. Yet, neither had Miss Hayhurst's willowy grace, more reminiscent of Arthur's own mother, what little he recalled of her.

Mrs. Barlow turned to Arthur. "And a good evening to you, Mr. Garrick."

"And to you, Mrs. Barlow," Arthur replied with a bow.

She offered a pleasant smile. "I thought we might play a hand or so of whist while we wait for Wendy to grace us with her presence?"

"A splendid idea, Mother," Wendel said, tone touched with surprise. "I hadn't considered that advantage to an additional house guest. Be my partner, Cousin Daphne?"

Mrs. Barlow extended a hand to her niece. "I rather thought gentlemen against ladies."

Wendel shrugged. "If you enjoy being trounced, Mother."

Mrs. Barlow's smile widened slightly but she didn't refute Wendel as she led the way to the card table. Once seated, she proffered the deck to her son and Wendel proceeded to shuffle and deal. Arthur found his hostess's pleasant, open expression somewhat disconcerting. He'd never seen this side of Mrs. Barlow before.

In all his visits, Arthur hadn't once sat down to cards with her. She'd always been an indifferent hostess, more concerned with avoiding her husband than catering to guests. As Wendel and Wendy had enjoyed their father's company, even as he'd declined, Mrs. Barlow had been little seen.

It took only a few rounds for Arthur to realize how outmatched he and Wendel were. A fair player, perhaps slightly better than Wendel, Arthur had never felt at such a disadvantage. Mrs. Barlow and Miss Hayhurst seemed almost to read each other's thoughts. Both played with alacrity and skill. Arthur could only be relieved that no money was on the line.

Finally, Wendel threw down his cards with a chuckle.

"No more, I beg you. My fragile pride cannot take another trouncing."

"Another trouncing at what?" Wendy asked, sweeping into the room. "Cards, Mother?"

For some reason her tone conveyed condemnation, though Arthur had no notion what could be condemned about whist. Especially as they didn't even gamble. Still, he tossed his hand on the table and pushed back his chair. It didn't do not to bow when Wendy entered a room. Around him, two other chairs pushed back. Mrs. Barlow remained seated, gathering the cards.

"Yes, Mother is playing cards, and she and Cousin Daphne trounced me and Garrick well-nigh to death." Wendel offered his sister a perfunctory bow.

Arthur provided a deeper, more reverent obeisance, then straightened to study his future bride. Wendy stood in the center of the parlor, directly under the chandelier. Candlelight sparkled off her golden locks, curled, piled high and strewn with decorations ranging from gems and lace to feathers and flowers. Below her powder laden blue eyes, rouged cheeks and red-dyed lips, the neckline of her dark pink gown plunged to almost obscene depths, showing off those curves that usually so beguiled him. On her left hip, a dark gray bow gathered the fabric of her dress, enhancing more curves. The overall effect was stunning. Any man would be proud to have her on his arm and would surely garner looks of envy. Wendy would never be one to enter a room unobtrusively and quietly play cards… as Miss Hayhurst had done.

Wendy extended a ring laden hand. "And this must be our cousin, Miss Hayhurst. Come, child, let me take a look at you."

"Child?" Amusement lurked in Miss Hayhurst's tone. "We're of an age, Cousin."

"Are we? You are not the younger sister, the one who has but seventeen years?" Wendy looked Miss Hayhurst up and down. "But, you're dressed like a child."

"Wendy." Mrs. Barlow snapped the deck of cards down on the table.

"Well, she is, Mother." Wendy turned back to Miss Hayhurst. "You can't possibly mean to make your come out in such gowns."

"This is one of my favorites," Miss Hayhurst replied with a calm Arthur recognized as similar to her aunt's, something she must get from her mother. "I enjoy dressing as the country Miss I am, but I must say you look stunning, Cousin."

Wendy stood straighter. "Thank you." She gave Miss Hayhurst a long, considering look. "You are correct, of course. It wouldn't do for you to attempt to look like more than you are." Her blue eyes narrowed. "Speaking of which, in whose conveyance did you arrive?"

Miss Hayhurst frowned. "My father's."

"Hmm. I must have seen a different carriage about."

"I wouldn't know enough to speak to that, Cousin."

Wendy offered a condescending smile. "No. You wouldn't." She turned to Arthur. "Come, Mr. Garrick, escort me to the dining room."

Arthur hurried forward, aware of Wendel offering an arm each to his mother and cousin. As Wendy walked beside him down the somewhat shabby corridor of the Barlows' country manor, Arthur didn't derive his usual satisfaction from the view down the front of her gown. He couldn't help but consider how Mrs. Barlow had never acted like a proper hostess before that evening. Never once, to his knowledge, for her husband. Wendy, like her mother, had a propensity for forming dislikes. Once they were wed and settled in London, would Wendy be a proper hostess for him, or follow the example set by Mrs. Barlow?

He wouldn't truly care, except that his younger sister would come out that Season, and Lillian would require not only a hostess and chaperone, but a mentor. He darted a glance at Wendy's daring décolletage. Arthur had longed to possess Wendy Barlow for years, but would she fill all the roles he required of her?

Chapter Four

Daphne hurried her steps, eager to breakfast with her aunt and Mr. Garrick. She'd been at the Barlows' for less than a week but had already discerned where she stood. Her aunt adored her, obviously trying to make up for years of separation. Cousin Wendel and Mr. Garrick were both polite and entertaining, if a bit condescending, but only Mr. Garrick would be awake as early as Daphne and Aunt Barlow. Wendel would sleep until nearly noon, as would Cousin Wendy… who outright despised Daphne.

Daphne hadn't any notion why. She tried to be polite. She attempted conversation. She ignored numerous slights and unending condescension. It was as if Cousin Wendy had determined a dislike before they'd even met.

Oft thought on, her father's parting wisdom replayed in Daphne's mind. The day she'd finished altering her yellow gown, when both Edward and Christine had been reprimanded, Daphne's father had also had words for her. Most were of love and assurance, letting her know that she could return early if need be.

The last, though, said with a hand braced on each of her shoulders, remained clearest in her mind: "Whatever you do, do not change who you are to suit them. I once endeavored to please a

Barlow. I transformed into a man I did not recognize and have wished ever after to forget. It nearly cost me your mother. A touch more idiocy and it could have cost a life. Do not be the fool I was. Do not permit them to make you doubt the worth of who you are."

She'd never seen her father as fierce as when he'd spoken those words. After that, she'd been nearly afraid to come to the Barlows' country seat. Now, she knew better what her father meant. If she catered to Wendy and flattered her, as Mr. Garrick did, her cousin would become amiable. Daphne understood the temptation. Everyone would get on better if she simply kowtowed to Wendy, but with her father's warning firmly in mind, Daphne refused to alter her nature to please her cousin.

Breakfast was served in a cheery sage parlor that flooded with sunlight each morning. Experience told Daphne that the room would be dark by the time her cousins made their way downstairs, and the food cold. Daphne, in contrast, strode into a room awash with sunlight and the delicious scents of breakfast. A glance showed she'd beaten her aunt down, but not Mr. Garrick.

"Good morning, Miss Hayhurst," he said, rising from his place at the table.

"Good morning, Mr. Garrick."

She turned to the sideboard in an effort to avoid his gaze without giving offense. Whenever she looked Mr. Garrick's way, those stormy gray eyes were fixed on her, generally over a slight frown. Daphne found his continuous scrutiny disconcerting, and unnecessary. She was hardly that interesting and he already intimidated, with his strong features and his wavy midnight hair. He didn't need to add continuous examination to augment the effect.

"Should I send for a pot of tea for you?" Mr. Garrick asked behind her, chair legs sliding along the floor as he retook his seat.

"Yes, thank you." Daphne glanced over her shoulder at the waiting maid. "A large one, please. I'm sure my aunt will join us soon."

At least, she hoped so. Mr. Garrick's company was perfectly bearable so long as at least one other person was about.

"There is a splendid currant jelly," Mr. Garrick continued. "Quite sour. I believe, your first morning here, you mentioned a preference for it."

"I did," Daphne replied, surprised that he recalled.

Out of consideration for the news, she selected an extra bun and then, with no more reason not to sit, turned from the sideboard and took the seat opposite Mr. Garrick, leaving the head of the table for her aunt.

Daphne placed a napkin in her lap, her gaze on her plate. The maid returned and began setting out cream and sugar, then disappeared again. Daphne took up a fork, trying not to feel Mr. Garrick's stare.

"Here." He pushed a small crystal bowl across the table. "I already sampled it. It's very good."

"Thank you." She risked a glance up to find

those clear gray eyes on her. She spooned a heap of jelly onto her plate and broke open a roll, the sound of crust cracking seeming overloud in the silence.

Mr. Garrick took a sip of coffee. "I hear tell that you and your younger sister will share a Season."

Daphne nodded. "Yes, although Christine isn't very keen on the idea."

"No?"

She shook her head. "My sister's heart is already engaged."

"Then why take on the expense of a Season?" A glance showed his frown deeper than usual.

Daphne shrugged. "I believe Father and Mother wish to be certain that her affection will hold. They feel that she must experience London before making her choice."

"That sounds reasonable. Your sister can't have met many gentlemen out in the countryside as you've always been."

Daphne offered a second shrug and risked another glance at his too-handsome face, keenly aware of how her heartbeat sped up each time she did. "I wouldn't say that. Father throws at least three balls a year. Everyone for miles attends."

A line appeared to mar Mr. Garrick's perfect brow. "He throws at least three balls a year?"

"One for the Yuletide, of course. Another each spring and one in the autumn. In the summer they hold a garden party instead. It's simply too hot for a ball. He and mother love to entertain."

Mr. Garrick's eyebrows crept up.

Daphne couldn't fathom why. Were four events

a year too many or too few by his London standards?

The maid bustled back in, laboring under a large pot of tea. Daphne welcomed the interruption as the young woman placed the pot on the table and bustled about with cups, spoons, and saucers.

It must be that four events a year seemed too few for Mr. Garrick's taste, shaped by time in London. To ensure that he didn't think her family painfully boring, she hastened to add, "And, of course, we have many smaller gatherings. Teas, dinners, picnics, hunts, recitals and the like. I'm sure nothing to compare to a busy London schedule, but we keep ourselves entertained."

"Evidently you do."

Now, what had she said to make him sound so confused? Daphne frowned as she reached for the tea. Perhaps a change of subject. "Have you any siblings, Mr. Garrick?"

"I do. A younger sister, Lillian. She's to have her come out this Season."

Daphne smiled. "Well then, we will undoubtedly have the pleasure of meeting her. Your mother will chaperone?" She envisioned his mother as tall, like him, and austerely elegant.

He shook his head. "We have lost both our parents and, until recently, been wards of my uncle. Now, however, I am of age and Lillian is my ward."

"My condolences to you both for your loss," Daphne murmured. "Your aunt will chaperone, then?"

Another shake of those impossibly dark locks.

"My uncle never wed. Lillian had a nanny but, when I came of age, Uncle Garrick released her. Since then, my sister has been installed in a finishing school in Derbyshire. It is now my responsibility to find for her both chaperone and confidante." He glanced at the empty doorway with a frown.

"You mean Cousin Wendy," Daphne said. "That is why you wish to wed before the Season."

His head snapped back around. "Who told you that?"

Her maid had, after speaking with the household staff, but something in his tone forbade incriminating the girl. "It's common knowledge in the household, sir."

"Yes, well, it's true. I've written to my uncle, informing him of my decision. I merely await his blessing to propose."

Daphne nodded, seeking about for another change of subject. Each one seemed more prickly than the last. "We're getting ready for the Season as well. Mother will take Christine and me to London early to procure new wardrobes." Daphne offered a self-effacing smile. "Apparently, my countrified garb will not suit the London crowd."

His gaze raked over her frame. "I find your attire refreshing."

Cheeks heating, she reached for the teapot to interrupt his gaze. Her hands shook as she poured. She could only hope that if he noticed, he would ascribe the weakness to the weight of the pot.

She returned the pot to the tabletop with a

thunk. She must master her reaction to Mr. Garrick. It was one thing not to bow to Cousin Wendy's will. Quite another to make calf-eyes at her beau. "Yes, well, Mother assures me that the ton will not be so forgiving as you, Mr. Garrick."

"So forgiving of what?" Aunt Barlow asked, entering the room. She rounded the table on Daphne's side and Mr. Garrick came to his feet. Aunt Barlow's hands settled on Daphne's shoulders. "Are you telling my niece frightful stories of London, Mr. Garrick?"

Mr. Garrick bowed where he stood. "Good morning, Mrs. Barlow."

Daphne craned her neck to look up at her aunt as Mr. Garrick sat. "No, Aunt. I'm telling him horrific tales about how Christine and I must endure fittings for entirely new wardrobes."

Aunt Barlow tweaked Daphne's nose, then continued to the head of the table to take her place. "Indeed, you must. A young woman as lovely as you must be clad in every new fashion and shown off to best advantage. I wouldn't be surprised if you win a member of the peerage, my dear."

Daphne shook her head. "I'll be content with a good man who loves me, and Christine is sure she's already found the gentleman of her dreams. I do think Mother is looking forward to the Season, though. She and Father haven't been to London since before I was born."

"No, they have not," Aunt Barlow agreed, words oddly clipped, then a smile brightened her face. "I see you've already ordered tea. How thoughtful."

"Allow me," Mr. Garrick said. "I believe the pot is rather full."

So, he had noticed Daphne's shaking hands. She fought down a blush.

Aunt Barlow emitted a sigh.

"What thoughtful young people both of you are. Not what I'm accustomed to."

A frown tugged at Mr. Garrick's lips, but he quickly schooled it away. His gaze lifted, gray eyes meeting Daphne's. She offered a slight shrug. From what her maid reported, Mr. Garrick knew the Barlows far better than she.

Aunt Barlow turned to the maid and requested a plate, then focused a keen look on Daphne. "Now, who is this gentleman who has captured Christine's heart before she can even have a Season?"

Daphne smiled, at ease with speaking about Ryan Quincy. A few years her senior, and possessed of three younger sisters with whom Daphne and her siblings were close, Mr. Quincy had been a friend to her family for nearly all her years.

"His name is Mr. Quincy. He is the second son of our nearest neighbor. He'd taken a commission and was a lieutenant on the front, but he sold out after his older brother died without an heir. He has three younger sisters. One a year younger than I am, one Christine's age, and one a year older than my younger brother Franklin. Mr. Quincy is a kind and practical gentleman, and I believe his attachment to Christine is as firm and genuine as possible."

"Yet, your parents insist that Christine have a Season?" Aunt Barlow asked, nodding to the maid as she set down a plate of food.

Daphne drew in a breath. Though Mr. Quincy's financial situation was common knowledge in the countryside about his estate, telling her aunt and Mr. Garrick seemed like gossiping. Instead, she said, "They insist that she know more of the world before making a decision."

Aunt Barlow nodded. "Yes, they would. That was the error your father made. One of them. Please pass that jelly, dear. Dare I hope it's currant?"

Daphne saw her keen interest mirrored in Mr. Garrick's face but could think of no graceful way to pursue the subject of her father's past mistakes. She handed her aunt the jelly. "Yes, it's currant."

"How odd. We do not keep currants. One of our tenants does, but she didn't gift us any this past season."

"She didn't?" Daphne blinked at the jelly, realizing she'd yet to try it. "Then how does it come to be here?"

"I haven't the faintest notion." Aunt Barlow spooned a large glob onto her plate, then smeared some on a bun and took a bite. "Definitely hers."

"I happened to mention the lack on my ride a few days past," Mr. Garrick said. "I'd stopped to water my mount."

Daphne avoided his eye, instead slathering jelly onto the bread she'd torn up earlier. A few days back? Did he mean before she'd arrived and mentioned a preference for currant jelly, or after? She popped a piece of bread into her mouth and found the jelly every bit as delectable as reported.

"That was good of you, Mr. Garrick. I daresay you know our tenants better than Wendel does."

Mr. Garrick shook his head. "I'm certain that is not the case, Mrs. Barlow. I simply find occasion to speak with them on my morning rides."

Aunt Barlow turned to Daphne. "Mr. Garrick routinely rises early. To stave off boredom, he rides out nearly every morning while Wendel and Wendy lounge about, not bothering to wake before noon."

"I daresay they're practicing for late nights in London," Mr. Garrick said lightly.

"You're too good a friend to them," Aunt Barlow replied.

Daphne sought about for another change of topic, unsure how the conversation had become so derailed that morning. Perhaps one of Shakespeare's tragedies? They'd had a very convivial discussion of Macbeth the previous day.

"You said younger brother, Miss Hayhurst?" Mr. Garrick's voice interrupted her thoughts. "I also believe you've mentioned another brother, Edward. How many siblings have you?"

"She has six," Aunt Barlow said. "Daphne, Edward, Christine, Franklin, Irving, Justina and Katherine, and all the boys the image of their father and the girls of my sister, except Daphne."

Mr. Garrick turned to her with a questioning look. "Oh?"

"I resemble my father." Daphne raised a hand to her brown hair. "I am not blessed with blonde curls and light-colored eyes like my mother, aunt, cousin and sisters."

"It's a shame I wasn't there for you in your youth, dear," Mrs. Barlow said. "I would have advised your mother to coat your hair in a mixture of lemon and honey, then have you sit out without a bonnet. You would be as blonde as the rest of us."

"Miss Hayhurst's hair is the color of honey," Mr. Garrick said. "That dark honey from the heart of the black forest. I warrant none would protest that being desirable."

"See how kind he is?" Aunt Barlow said. "I know," she continued before Daphne could form a response. "You should go riding with Mr. Garrick this morning, dear. See some of the countryside hereabouts. You've been very kind to spend your mornings with me, but I am rather out of sorts today. I'm afraid I am not good company."

"Oh." Daphne blinked. "If you prefer, Aunt, but I'm happy to bear you company if my presence will please you."

Aunt Barlow shook her head. "It would, certainly, but that wouldn't be fair to you. It is no fault of yours that I have let so much bitterness into my heart over the years." She let out a sigh. "Normally, to look on you brings me joy. Today, all I see are years squandered." She rose from the table, causing them both to rise as well. "You and Mr. Garrick have a pleasant ride."

Aunt Barlow sailed from the room.

Daphne turned to Mr. Garrick but saw him unsurprised by her aunt's behavior. Did that mean Aunt Barlow was prone to such fits? Regardless, it would be inappropriate for Daphne to ride out with the man her cousin admired or to ignore her aunt's need for cheering, let alone do both at once.

"Please do not take offense, but I will not ride with you. Despite my aunt's protests, I will endeavor to comfort her."

"That would be for the best."

Daphne tried to ignore her disappointment that he'd agreed so readily and retook her seat. She resolved to concentrate on her food, keenly aware that any time she did look up, it would be to meet his cool gray eyes.

Chapter Five

Seated at a small table in the Barlows' back parlor, Arthur frowned as Wendy played yet another useless card. Beside him, Miss Hayhurst laid hers down with a grin.

"We win again," Wendel crowed, reaching for the tally sheet.

Wendy tossed the remnants of her hand onto the table. "How is it that they keep beating us, Mr. Garrick? I always supposed you good at cards."

"He'd have to be downright brilliant to carry you, sister dear," Wendel said with a chuckle as he tallied the points. "Besides which, it's not Garrick's fault our cousin excels at cards."

Wendy's eyes took on a dangerous glint.

"It's simply a question of luck," Arthur temporized. "They've been dealt better hands."

"Every round?" Wendel raised his eyebrows.

Arthur gave him a repressive look. As they reached the middle of April, the weather had turned. The back parlor, where Wendy still insisted on a fire, held a closed-in stuffiness that made Arthur's head pound, a condition not improved by repeatedly losing at cards. One which would be made much worse if Wendy fell into a temper, especially a temper which involved screeching.

Wendy tipped her nose into the air. "Wendel dealt that hand. He likely cheated."

"Mr. Garrick may be correct," Miss Hayhurst inserted when Wendel looked up from his tallying. "It may simply be a question of luck."

Arthur noticed that she'd said 'may' twice. He took that to mean that she didn't believe it to be luck at all. Why should she? She possessed an exemplary quickness of wit, visible the moment one looked into her almond shaped amber eyes.

Wendel snorted. "Aye, and Cousin Daphne is also lucky at chess, I suppose. I noticed that she, by mere chance, beat you two out of three matches yesterday, Garrick."

Eyes narrowed to bright slits of anger, Wendy turned a glare on her cousin. "You played chess with Mr. Garrick? When was this?"

"Leave off, Wendy," Wendel said as he tossed slate and chalk onto the table. "We have to entertain ourselves somehow while we wait for you to show up for dinner. It's not Daphne's fault that you were nearly two hours late last evening. Cook had a fit, you know."

"And I should care what our cook thinks?" Wendy's voice held a shrill note.

"May I insert that you were well worth the wait," Arthur interjected. "You looked amazing yesterday evening. Any man in London would be lucky to have you on his arm, for every other gentleman would boil with envy."

"Until they dealt with the sharp side of her tongue," Wendel muttered.

Wendy's burgeoning smile tipped back down into a frown.

"Excuse me sirs, misses." Relief swept through Arthur as he turned to see the Barlows' butler in the doorway. "Pardon the interruption, but a letter has arrived for Mr. Garrick, from Mr. Oscar Garrick, for which I believe Mr. Garrick has been waiting."

Arthur sprang to his feet and met the butler halfway across the room. "Thank you." He plucked the letter from the tray. "I'd started to worry that he wouldn't reply in time."

Wendy appeared at his shoulder. "Read it to me."

"I planned to read it to you on your birthday."

"That's nearly two weeks away. Read it to me now."

Arthur couldn't suppress a grin, finding Wendy's eagerness flattering. He cracked open his uncle's seal and unfolded the thick paper.

"'To my most obedient nephew'," he read and shook his head. "As if he has any other nephews."

"I believe he simply means that you are most obedient, not the most obedient," Miss Hayhurst offered.

"Shush," Wendy snapped. "Arthur, read on. Did he agree to increase your allowance when we wed? By how much? Will he send a wedding gift?"

"'To my most obedient nephew'," he began again. "'I have given your plan to propose to Miss Barlow all due consideration. I realize that you seek my blessing and I did not miss your unsubtle demand for greater monthly funds.'" Arthur winced. He'd thought his request perfectly subtle.

"He sounds grouchy," Wendy said.

"He's always grouchy." Arthur cleared his throat and continued. "'My response to both is no.'" Arthur blinked. He read the line again.

"What does he mean, 'no'?" Wendy asked.

Arthur turned to look down at her, the pounding in his head redoubling. "He means he does not give us his blessing and will not increase my allowance."

Wendy gasped. "How vile. What a terrible old man. Does that mean we must wait for him to die before we can live as we ought? He's been ill, hasn't he?"

Arthur nodded, feeling a bit numb. He'd never for a moment considered that his uncle might refuse him.

"Does he say why not?" Miss Hayhurst's calm, quiet voice asked from somewhere behind Arthur.

"I… I don't know."

Would they have to wait for his uncle to die to procure more funds? Uncle Garrick had suffered ill health for years but never showed any indication of passing. Nor did Arthur wish him to. After the carriage accident that had robbed him and Lillian of their parents, Uncle Garrick was all they had. He'd raised Arthur from the time he was seven and Lillian but three.

"Give me that." Wendy snatched the letter from Arthur's hands. "'My most obedient,'" she muttered, gaze skimming over the page. "It says here, 'I've tolerated your association with the Barlows on the assumption that the lad cannot possibly be as bad as his father, and that you would outgrow your infatuation with the lass. As you have not, I must inform you that if you wed Miss Barlow, you will be cut off. Not only while I live, but always. I will alter my will and leave everything to the Church. Mr. Hayhurst has long been a valued associate of mine and I will not see a penny of my fortune, which he assisted me in amassing, go to a Barlow. Think on that, and then decide if you still love her.'"

Wendy looked up from the page, slack jawed.

"What does he mean, not as bad as his father?" Wendel asked.

Arthur turned to him, dazed. "I don't know." He rubbed his forehead. "I know all of London took sides in whatever transpired between Mr. Hayhurst and your father. They say it was the scandal of the Season."

"A Season over two decades ago," Wendel protested.

Wendy whirled, page crumpling in her hands, to glare at Miss Hayhurst. "This is your fault," she snarled.

Miss Hayhurst's eyebrows shot up. "Mine?"

"You and your horrible family. I don't know why you were driven out of London, but I'm sure my father was right to do it."

Miss Hayhurst stared at her. "We weren't driven out of London."

"Oh yes, that's right, you're too poor to go, even if you'd be permitted."

"Too poor?" Miss Hayhurst shook her head.

"And you." Wendy whirled back to face Arthur.

"How could you lead me on in this fashion? How could you let me squander years making eyes at you, working to please only you, when you have no intention of wedding me? At least now I know why you would not kiss me in the garden." Her arm snaked out.

Slap!

Arthur's head snapped back, more from surprise than the force of the blow. A prickling, stinging sensation spread across his cheek.

"If I were a man, I would challenge you, Arthur Garrick." Wendy whirled again, this time to her brother. "Wendel, challenge him. Shoot him for me."

Arthur rubbed his face. "Miss Barlow, Wendy, please. You misunderstand. I still mean for us to marry."

She spun back, making Arthur dizzy on her behalf. "What?"

Taking in her regal countenance, her flashing sapphire eyes, Arthur sucked in a breath and dropped to a knee. "Miss Barlow, agree to be my wife."

"You are still asking me to marry you? Even though you will lose everything?"

"Of course I am. It is the only honorable course. I have a few thousand pounds invested and your dowry is two thousand more. With that, we can have an income of two hundred a year." He made a sweeping gesture. "We won't have a manor like this, but my parents had a cottage in—"

"No," Wendy snapped, interrupting him. "A

cottage, Mr. Garrick? Don't be absurd. That is out of the question."

Arthur blinked up at her, confused. "I don't understand."

"Let me be clearer, then." Wendy's voice crackled with frost. "Mr. Garrick, I will absolutely not marry you. Two hundred pounds a year. Don't be ridiculous. That is not the life I plan to live."

"But… that is… I…" Arthur shook his head. "I love you."

"But I do not love you." She drew her shoulders back, magnificent in her fury. "You can take your uncle's letter and his fortune and remove yourself from my life, Mr. Garrick." She dropped the crumpled ball that was his uncle's letter on the floor in front of him. "Now, if you will excuse me, my correspondences require my immediate attention. I have a Season for which to prepare, so I can find a worthwhile gentleman." Whirling again, she swept from the room.

Arthur stared after her, unable to muster a proper thought. His other knee hit the floor beside the first. Distantly, someone called his name.

"…elp me get him up," a voice said somewhere behind him.

Hands clasped his arms. Dimly, he registered that the two wrapped about his left arm were long-fingered and small, while his right arm was seized in a strong grip. Both sets of hands yanked. Arthur came to his feet.

"Come on, to the sofa. Daphne, there's brandy on the sideboard."

One set of hands disappeared as the other half-dragged Arthur to a sofa and shoved him down to sit. Miss Hayhurst appeared, glass in hand. She dropped to a knee before him and held it out, expression worried.

"Drink up, Garrick," Wendel's voice said, but Arthur couldn't pull his gaze away from Miss Hayhurst's magnetic amber eyes.

"Here." Her voice was soft, as were her hands when she took his and wrapped them about the hard crystal of the glass.

"Come on, Garrick. Just a sip," Wendel coaxed. "There you go. Now another."

Miss Hayhurst looked over her shoulder, exposing a length of elegant neck. "Do you think she means it?" she asked Wendel.

Wendel shrugged. "She sounded as if she meant it."

Arthur took another swig of brandy. It burned more than Wendy's slap had.

"She was shocked, is all," Miss Hayhurst protested to Wendel. "She'll come around. Two hundred pounds a year is enough, and they can visit here, I assume, and wherever Miss Garrick ends up living, to take some of the strain off their finances."

"Would you wed a gentleman who could only offer you two hundred pounds a year?" Wendel asked.

Miss Hayhurst nodded. "If I loved him, certainly. I would wed him with less. That is why I know Cousin Wendy will come to her senses."

"I don't believe Wendy ever takes leave of her

senses," Wendel said.

Miss Hayhurst turned back to Arthur, expression worried.

He took another swallow of brandy but found his glass dry. "She said no."

"More brandy?" Wendel asked uncertainly.

Arthur rarely drank. He shook his head. "No."

"What will you do?" Miss Hayhurst still knelt before him, features clouded with concern.

Arthur handed her the empty glass and sat up straighter. "I will win her back. What else is there to do?" He turned to Wendel. "Or am I no longer welcome here?"

Wendel snorted. "You're my friend, Garrick. You were before you met my sister and you still are now. In fact, we will have a better time of it, now that you no longer have to cater to her."

Miss Hayhurst came to her feet in a fluid motion, dusting off her skirt with her free hand. "But he will, if he's to win her back."

"Yes, well, he won't have to this moment," Wendel said firmly. "Therefore, I say we get out of this stuffy parlor and go for a ride."

"Agreed." Arthur came to his feet. The room swayed slightly, though whether from the brandy or shock, he didn't know.

Miss Hayhurst took a half step back, looking between Wendel and him, a question clear in her eyes.

"Would you like to accompany us, Cousin Daphne?"

A tentative smile curved her bowlike lips. "If

you're certain I will not be in the way."

"Do we have to let you win if we race?" Wendel asked.

She shook her head vigorously, the glint in her eyes giving Arthur the impression that they not only wouldn't have to let her win, but would be lucky if they could best her.

"Will you ride slowly and insist on speaking without interruption?" Wendel pressed.

Another shake of those caramel curls.

"What if there's mud," Arthur asked in a nearly normal tone, attempting to join the spirit of the game. "Will you make us ride around it or may we press through?"

"You may press through. I will endeavor to jump over."

Yes, for certain, that gleam in her gaze spoke of a challenge. This wouldn't be like the morning her aunt had suggested they take a ride, when Miss Hayhurst declined in favor of keeping Mrs. Barlow company. A lurking madness swirled through Arthur. That was what he required. Running. Jumping. A challenge. Something to burn away the confusion and shame that clenched his gut.

Refreshed, he would return and confront Wendy. He would remind her that he was a man first, the man she'd fallen in love with, and the heir to his uncle's fortune second.

Chapter Six

Daphne took one more glance about the empty meadow. Sheltered by a hillock on each side, the wildflower strewn valley lay near the Barlows' manor but out of sight. That closeness imparted enough assurance to allow her to venture out alone, while the valley offered enough privacy for one of her favorite occupations… dancing.

She hadn't danced with a partner even once since arriving at her cousins' home. They seemed to have no friends or acquaintances other than Mr. Garrick, and never attended events or made calls. Since the arrival of his uncle's letter almost two weeks ago, even Mr. Garrick's company put a strain on the household. So, as a secret joy, Daphne had begun coming out to the meadow each morning after breakfast, to dance.

Not only did she miss dancing, she feared she'd suffer from a lack of practice. She would come out that autumn. In less than six months, all of London would see her dance, so she must practice. If her only means of practicing was to dance alone, then she would. Not that she minded much. The meadow proved a lovely place to dance.

That morning, as she was a touch earlier than usual, shadows still draped the valley floor. Many of the wildflowers had drawn closed in the night. Dew and a slight chill lingered, but Daphne knew she wouldn't be cold once she started. She selected a location in the center of the meadow, began humming the melody, assumed the proper position, and danced.

Lightness filled her. The sun crested the valley to stream down, touching wildflowers that created a pattern more intricate than any carpet crafted in the Orient. A strong breeze sprang up, lending a chill to the late April air. Her body twirled and leaped as commanded. She couldn't help but smile, something she would remember not to permit on the London dance floor. Her mother had warned her, often enough, that in London, a lady guarded her emotions.

Daphne executed the final spin, then dropped a low curtsy, slightly out of breath. In her enthusiasm, she'd quite possibly completed the dance in double time. Another mistake to guard against when she began her Season.

The sound of clapping spun her about. Mr. Garrick stood near the top of the hill that sheltered the valley from the manor, but when she sighted him, he started down. Daphne's cheeks heated with more than exertion. She pulled her shoulders back and crossed to meet him, the smile on his face a welcome sight, even if it came at her expense.

"I did not realize I had an audience," she said when they met on the valley floor.

"Nor did I realize I might witness such a display."

Her cheeks burned a bit brighter. "A gentleman would have announced his presence or walked on."

Levity fled his features. "I daresay you are correct, Miss Hayhurst. I beg leave to apologize."

Daphne pursed her lips. She'd only meant to tease. "I do not grant you leave, sir. In truth, you've nothing for which to be sorry."

Gray eyes perused her frame and Daphne fought down a fresh blush. Mr. Garrick held out a hand. "You dance well, Miss Hayhurst, but seem in want of a partner."

Daphne stared at his hand in surprise. Did she dare take it? Dare to let this undeniably appealing gentleman stand close? But then, Mr. Garrick was so in love with Wendy, what harm could there be?

His offer was a kindness, not a flirtation. She must view dancing with him as she would dancing with Mr. Quincy. Not a relation, but a friend longstanding enough to be nearly one.

Daphne placed her hand in Mr. Garrick's. Heat shot up her arm. His palm proved less smooth than she would have imagined a gentleman's hands to be, his grip firm as he closed his fingers about hers. She wondered if she should insist that they stop, for lack of gloves. Before she could decide, he led them back to where she'd begun her dance.

He turned to face her, not relinquishing her hand. "And what do you wish to practice, Miss Hayhurst?"

Heat radiated up her arm and filled her. "I'm not certain."

As always, he studied her, expression thoughtful. "You already seem quite accomplished in the realm of the country reel. Perhaps something more obscure, to prepare you if called on?"

"Such as?"

"What of a minuet?"

A minuet seemed safe enough. A dance from her parents' time. She'd feared he would suggest something scandalous, like this new waltz of which she'd heard whispers. "I have not danced a minuet in ages."

"Well then, we will practice. You never know when you may be called upon to attempt one."

Bemused, Daphne nodded. Mr. Garrick bowed over her hand, then began the count. Movements strong and sure, he led them into the dance.

She'd performed the steps hundreds of times. As a child, she'd loved to watch her parents dance thus, as they had been that fateful Yuletide night, the first time she'd sneaked from bed to peer through the railing at one of their balls. Her mother in a confection of pale yellow. Her father tall and slim, clad in powdery blue. Her parents had glided over the dance floor in perfect harmony.

Much as she and Mr. Garrick moved now, sunlight warm about them and the sky a deep blue above. His strong hands conveyed complete assurance in the steps, engulfing her smaller ones each time they clasped. About them, wildflowers began to unfold in the morning light. Soon, the floor and walls of the valley were awash in a sea of colors. The air filled with a sweet scent.

And then he drew them into a final turn. His deep voice, almost like music with his steady count, silenced. He bowed over her hand again, this time brushing her knuckles with his lips.

Lightning seemed to speed up her arm. Daphne gasped.

He raised concerned gray eyes as he straightened. "Are you unwell, Miss Hayhurst?"

"I—no."

He pressed her fingers a final time and released them. "Thank you for a lovely dance. A moment of joy in what, of late, seems a bleak existence."

Daphne blinked rapidly, trying to find thoughts, to slow the pounding of her heart. "Bleak?"

Her gaze focused on his lips. They'd felt so soft, yet firm against her skin. Heart pounding even harder, she wrenched her attention back to his eyes. Fortunately, he looked past her, in the direction of the manor house.

"Miss Barlow's birthday is in two days. For years I thought…" He trailed off with a grimace. "I am unsure that I will win her over."

"You would truly give up everything for her?"

He met Daphne's gaze squarely. "I would."

"Why?" The word was out before she could call it back. Her cheeks flamed. "That is, what is it about Cousin Wendy?"

Did Daphne lack something? Some trait needed to inspire the sort of devotion her cousin inspired in Mr. Garrick? From another, of course. She had no desire to re-estrange their families.

He frowned, thoughtful, but for once his gaze avoided hers. "I'm not completely sure. When first we met, I did not care for her. She seemed spoiled, doted on by her father and sheltered by her brother.

Willful, as well." He shook his head. "Then, she seemed always about. Always offering a smile. Appearing wherever I was. I began to notice her… charms." A wry smile curved his lips.

"I realize it is not my place to say, but she hardly seems charming." Daphne studied his reaction through wide eyes, worried he would take offense.

Mr. Garrick nodded. "She has become more shrill of late. She did not take her father's decline and passing well. She does not get on with Mrs. Barlow." He pressed a hand through his wavy charcoal locks, disheveling them. "She has grown more demanding. Perhaps because her father always showered her with attention and gifts."

"Perhaps." To Daphne, Cousin Wendy seemed rather terrible, and not at all worthy of Mr. Garrick's devotion. "Maybe she is simply being dramatic, to test your love?"

"Maybe."

"Or, could your uncle simply be testing her love, and yours?"

Mr. Garrick frowned. Hope flickered in his gaze, then died. "No. My uncle is not the sort. He meant every word of his letter." Squaring broad shoulders, Mr. Garrick stood straighter. "Regardless, I will make one more try, on her birthday. If she truly won't have me, then I must abide by her decision."

Daphne nodded. To her shame, she couldn't help but hope her cousin refused him again. Not because of his alluring gray eyes, or the way his touch sent heat shooting up her arm and through her frame, or because of how his lips on her hand had sparked shimmering lightning inside her. For his sake. Even if Daphne never set eyes on Mr. Garrick again, he deserved better than Cousin Wendy.

"I should return to the house." He frowned. "I do not mean to imply that anything inappropriate took place, but I cannot help but think it would be best if we did not arrive together."

Daphne tamped down another blush. Nothing improper had occurred. They'd simply danced. A minuet. An old-fashioned, inoffensive dance that their grandparents would have done. True, they'd done so without gloves, but hands were only hands. Her gaze shifted to his, loose at his sides. Long fingered and strong.

Mr. Garrick bowed. "I will see you within, Miss Hayhurst."

Daphne nodded, not sure of her voice. She tracked his progress as long legs carried him from the valley. Once he disappeared over the lip, she let out a groan and pressed her palms to her eyes. She'd never been infatuated with a gentleman. Why must her silly heart choose this one on whom to fixate? Every possibility existed that her cousin would accept his final offer of marriage.

Lowering her hands, she turned in a slow circle, taking in the sun-drenched valley. Honeybees buzzed among the flowers now, their gentle hum lulling. A wistful sigh left her lips. If she never saw Mr. Garrick again, at least she would forever have that morning's lovely memory.

She turned and trudged up the hill, following the path he'd made through the flowers. She'd need to change before joining the others in the parlor. Her hem was damp and dusted with pollen. Hopefully, her maid could clean the gown. Daphne hadn't brought many with her.

Cresting the hill brought the house into sight, along with a conflict of feelings. When she departed the Barlows' country estate, she would likely never see Mr. Garrick again, save in passing. Yet, she longed to depart. As kind as her aunt had turned out to be, as amiable as Mr. Garrick and Cousin Wendel could be if they so chose, Wendy's dislike colored nearly every interaction, every moment. Since her falling out with Mr. Garrick, Daphne's cousin had become nearly insufferable. On top of that, Daphne missed her parents, her brothers and sisters, and her home.

Daphne had nearly reached the kitchen door, planning to go from there up the back steps to her chamber, when it flew open to reveal Mr. Garrick. He hurried in her direction, his expression pinched with worry. Catching his mood, she quickened her steps.

"Whatever is amiss?" she called as she drew near. Had something happened to her aunt or one of her cousins?

"Your father's carriage has been and gone, seeking you. Everyone is searching for you."

"Father's carriage? Why?" Dread snaked through Daphne. She was scheduled to depart in less than a week. She couldn't imagine why her father would send for her early.

Mr. Garrick shook his head. "I didn't wait to hear the news. I came to fetch you. Come." He wheeled back to the house.

Daphne followed him inside and through the kitchen. She nearly had to run to keep pace with his stride as they traversed the wide, dim corridors. Finally, they burst into the front parlor, where her aunt paced while Cousin Wendy perched in an armchair, reading.

"Daphne." Aunt Barlow rushed forward. "Where have you been? Never mind that. There is news. Sit with me." She grabbed Daphne's arm and pulled her to the sofa.

"Aunt, whatever is the matter? Mr. Garrick said Father's carriage came and went?"

"Where were you?" Wendy asked. She regarded Daphne through narrowed eyes. "Your hem is sodden." Her gaze snapped to Mr. Garrick. "Like Mr. Garrick's boots."

"What's happened?" Daphne pressed, ignoring Wendy.

Pulling Daphne down to sit on the sofa, Aunt Barlow captured her hands. "Irving has fallen from a tree. He broke several bones, but worse than that, he remains unconscious. They do not know if he will ever wake again."

Daphne stared at her. "My brother Irving?"

"She could hardly mean a different Irving, or we wouldn't have scoured the house for you."

"Wendy," Aunt Barlow snapped, voice devoid of warmth, before turning back to Daphne. "Your father sent the carriage, but they couldn't remain. They're also tasked with bringing Edward home. The coachman said he'll return for you after Edward is delivered."

"But, that will take days. What if…" She trailed off, unable to utter the words. She swallowed against the hard lump in her throat. What if she never saw her youngest brother alive again? "He's only thirteen."

"Why are your boots wet?" Wendy aimed the question at Mr. Garrick, who stood immediately inside the parlor doorway.

"This is hardly the time," he replied, voice low.

"Perhaps your coachman could take me?" Daphne asked her aunt, tone pleading.

"Certainly not," Wendy snapped. "I require the carriage for my birthday."

Aunt Barlow pulled her hands free of Daphne's to turn a hard look on her daughter. "That is not your decision."

"No, but in two days it will be Wendel's decision."

"Then let him make it," Aunt Barlow said.

"He isn't here. He's riding about the grounds looking for her."

Daphne wrapped her arms about herself, her aunt and Wendy's sniping churning to a dull buzz in her ears. The pain swelling in her gut threatened to bring tears to her eyes. She closed them, but the moment they shut, an image of Irving in a tree, dangling a doll to taunt their little sisters, filled her vision.

Tears slipped down her cheeks.

"I will take Miss Hayhurst in my carriage," Mr. Garrick said.

Daphne's eyes flew open.

"You will what?" Wendy snapped.

"I will take Miss Hayhurst and her maid back to her family."

"Thank you." Daphne's words came out a whisper, but Mr. Garrick offered her a nod.

"Will you now?" Wendy asked, blue eyes glinting.

"That is very kind of you, Mr. Garrick," Aunt Barlow said.

Daphne blinked rapidly, shedding tears from her eyes. She swiped a hand over each cheek. "But you will miss Cousin Wendy's birthday."

"Apparently, he does not care," Wendy said crisply, sitting very straight in her armchair.

Mr. Garrick turned to her. "I do care but can similarly employ this moment." He crossed the room and, as he had nearly two weeks ago, dropped to a knee before her. "Miss Barlow, I am willing to forgo my uncle's fortune to be with you, if you are willing to forgo it to be with me. I've planned this proposal for years, but your father was ill and then you mourned him. Through all that, my dream has been to make you mine. Will you be my wife?"

Daphne could scarcely breathe. Not around the pain in her throat, nor past the hammering of her heart. Aunt Barlow watched with an open mouth and wide eyes, hands clutched to her chest.

Wendy frowned at Mr. Garrick, his face of a

height with hers as he knelt. "You may be able to live without your uncle's fortune, Mr. Garrick, but I refuse to."

Aunt Barlow gasped.

Mr. Garrick's mouth pulled down in a frown.

Wendy emitted a sigh. "You are very handsome, Arthur, and kind, though far too stodgy. I would have enjoyed the envy evidenced by other women when I attended events on your arm. Now, you cannot give me that. You have only two good qualities left to offer, and as kindness is worthless to me, really only one." She reached out and patted his cheek, her eyes flinty. "Do not worry for me. I have already set in motion new plans for my happiness. Take my chit of a cousin back to her family. I've no need of you anymore."

Aunt Barlow made a strangled sound.

Mr. Garrick levered to his feet, towering over Wendy. Expression hard, he turned to Daphne. "Make ready with all haste, Miss Hayhurst," he said and strode from the room.

Chapter Seven

Arthur paced the Hayhursts' library, trying not to be awed by the space. A long room, the fanciful bird, sky, and leaf pattern on the ceiling seemed the most light-hearted aspect. Certainly, the volumes packing the shelves between the tall, narrow windows were not. So far as he could ascertain, not a single gothic novel stood on the shelves, nor almost any literature or even poetry.

The Bard himself was relegated to a single set of books, located in a back corner.

Instead, volumes of scientific inquiry and knowledge abounded. Books on husbandry. Chemistry. Geography. The art of chess. Pure mathematics. Italian, French, Greek and Latin each had their own sections. The most frivolous of the lot, if they could even be labeled as such, were books pertaining to mythology, dance, and art.

Large, overstuffed sofas dotted the space, along with armchairs, but also tables set round with stiff wooden chairs and benches. Several of these were littered with candelabras and volumes. Arthur stopped beside one and, without losing the pages to which they lay open, half closed each book to read the titles. Mathematic and economic theories of application.

He peered at the formulas jotted down on several sheets of paper. Though university educated, he could make no sense of them.

One hand resting on the table beside those confusing figures, Arthur lifted his gaze to the nearest window. Without stood a huge, well manicured garden. Through various windows, he'd glimpsed artfully trimmed hedges, vast lawns, bubbling fountains, a veritable rainbow of flowers, and paths covered in crushed white marble.

What would Wendel and Wendy make of the room in which he stood? Of the entire house. They'd always maintained that their cousins were poor relations who would be annoying hangers on in London. They claimed that the Hayhursts didn't visit town because of the expense and because they required the income of renting out their London home, which was located on a very fashionable street, too much to reside there themselves.

Arthur shook his head. From the moment his carriage had turned up the tree-lined drive, it had been clear that the Hayhursts were very wealthy. The livery of the footmen and grooms who'd swarmed his carriage was nearly as fine as Arthur's garb. When he'd stepped free of his conveyance, the manor house had loomed vast and pristinely maintained, from the perfectly kept plantings to the granite gargoyles perched high above.

And Mrs. Hayhurst, a younger, lovelier version of Mrs. Barlow, had met him with all courtesy, polite even in her state of distress. Miss Hayhurst, as well, had maintained perfect civility during their journey and when they arrived, despite obvious strain. She had rushed off to see her brother, taking her mother with her, but not before asking what he required, offering to have victuals sent, and asking a servant to show him to his choice of either a parlor or the library. He couldn't imagine Wendy or Mrs. Barlow behaving with similar decorum.

Thinking on Wendy, Arthur slid into one of the chairs at the table. On their journey, he'd been a poorer companion than Miss Hayhurst. Arthur had spent the entirety of the two-day trip attempting to sort out his feelings.

Anger. Betrayal. Shock. A certain amount of embarrassment.

These were paramount, but also, to his shame, a touch of relief. He'd made a promise to Wendy Barlow, to Wendel and Mrs. Barlow as well, in essence. Though nothing had ever been made official, expectations were longstanding and clear. Honor had dictated that Arthur ask for Wendy's hand, as had his heart.

Or so he'd thought.

Yet, were his heart fully engaged, why a feeling of relief? Was he so shallow that he truly did prefer his uncle's money over the hand of the woman he loved? Or did something more stir him?

His gaze went to a large family portrait set over one of the room's fireplaces. The portrait depicted Mr. Hayhurst, whom Arthur had yet to meet, and Mrs. Hayhurst. They both smiled and were surrounded by seven children, the youngest a babe in arms. Arthur guessed the painting to be not quite a decade old. He grimaced, thoughts going to his own family, such as it was. Lillian would be eighteen next spring. He'd promised her a Season. Now, he had no chaperone. No one to introduce her about or return calls with her. Elbows braced on the table, he rubbed his forehead. When he got back to London, he would begin interviewing women for the role.

"Trying to steal my father's secrets?" a male voice asked behind him.

Arthur swiveled in the chair to find a young man with an angry expression striding through the library's open double doors. He rose to his feet and turned more fully, offering a bow.

"I beg your pardon, Mr.…?" Arthur paused, though the mid-brown curls were reminiscent of Daphne's caramel tresses and the hazel eyes mirrored Mrs. Hayhurst's blue ones, marking the man as Edward Hayhurst.

"Mr. Edward Hayhurst." He did not bow.

Arthur did, straightening to say, "Arthur Garrick."

If anything, Hayhurst's scowl deepened. "I know who you are. I've just come from visiting a friend in London. The ton is abuzz about you, Garrick."

Arthur mimicked the younger man's expression. "Me?" He hadn't been in London since the end of February. What could there be to talk about? "Perhaps you confuse me with another, Mr. Hayhurst?"

"I think not."

"May I then assume this purported talk is the impetus for what can only be called a lack of civility on your behalf?"

"You may." Hayhurst jabbed a finger at the library door. "You may also vacate this manor directly."

Arthur stiffened. "I do not believe that is for you to decide. I am a guest of your sister's." Why did the younger man insist on such hostility? "You do know that I brought her here?"

"I do, and I know why, and you cannot have her, Garrick."

Arthur's eyebrows shot up. "I beg your pardon?"

"Look, I'm sure you're a decent enough fellow, but I will not permit you to solve your financial woes through my sister. Daphne deserves someone who cares for her, not her dowry."

Garrick shook his head as if that might clear his ears of such confusing nonsense. "What financial woes?"

"Don't prevaricate, Garrick. I'm not a fool."

"Pretend I am and enlighten me."

Edward Hayhurst studied him with a frown. Finally, he said, "It's come out that you were after Wendy Barlow for her dowry and she found out as much and threw you over." He shrugged. "I understand a man needs a certain incentive to marry and that you have a sister to consider. It must have come as a shock to realize your uncle is pockets to let. We all thought him wealthy, if stodgy, what with that miserable little house on the edge of what's fashionable, firing your sister's companion, and sending her to a second-rate school. None of us realized how bad things are. That doesn't give you any right to come after Daphne's dowry, though." Hayhurst shook his head, expression perplexed. "How you found out about it, I'll never know. She doesn't even know what Father's settled on her."

"All that has come out?" Arthur said slowly. "In the past few weeks, I suppose?"

Edward Hayhurst nodded. "I'm only glad I was in town to hear about it. News never reaches us out here."

"Right," Arthur said, flabbergasted by the accusations.

"You understand, it's my duty to protect Daphne from your less than honorable suit?"

Arthur bit back a bitter chuckle. "Oh yes, I understand." He had no doubt where such malicious gossip got its start. To whom Wendy had first written, he would never know, but her lies had obviously spread like fire. Had Lillian heard such foul rumors yet? Would it affect her prospects?

Hayhurst's expression became a bit abashed. "You would do the same for your sister."

"Indeed." What Arthur needed to do for his sister was stem the tide of such lunacy.

"Then you'll go peaceably? No hard feelings?"

"I will. In fact, I will leave this moment. Give my regards to your mother and sister."

Edward Hayhurst grimaced. "I'd rather not."

Arthur ground his teeth together. "As you wish. Please excuse me."

"Right."

The younger man stepped out of the way as Arthur strode from the room.

Chapter Eight

Daphne checked the formal parlor but found it empty. Trying to press her unease for Irving to the back of her mind, she sought the library. That room, as well, showed no sign of Mr. Garrick. She returned to the entrance hall and waved over a footman.

"Was Mr. Garrick given a room?" She'd meant to offer him one, the hour rather late to begin the long ride to London, but didn't recall if, in her haste to see Irving, she had.

"A room? No, Miss. The gentleman departed some time ago."

Daphne blinked, confused. "He left?" Without bidding her farewell?

"Yes, Miss."

"Did he give a reason?" Had another calamity fallen?

"No, Miss."

How odd. "Thank you."

The footman nodded.

Daphne turned slowly, unsure where to go.

She'd left her mother and father at Irving's bedside. She didn't know if she could endure more of staring down at him, her whispered words seeming to have no effect at all, his oddly small looking form swaddled in blankets, one arm and one leg set in splints.

Why had Mr. Garrick left without executing proper civility? That didn't seem like him. True, he'd been quiet on their journey, hardly addressing her more often than he had her maid. She'd assumed he had much on his mind, and quiet and rude were not one and the same.

She'd looked forward to showing him about the manor and the grounds. She should especially have liked to see his reaction to the grand ballroom. The idea of, possibly, dancing with him there one day had been a bright spot in an otherwise dismal two days.

Footsteps sounded on the staircase. She looked up to see Edward descending.

"Have you any notion why Mr. Garrick left, Edward?"

Edward puffed out his chest. He reached the bottom step and said, "I got rid of him for you."

Daphne frowned. "What do you mean?"

"I ran him off. He can't be hanging about, eyes on your dowry."

At her sides, Daphne's hands curled into fists. "What do you mean? Mr. Garrick has no intentions regarding my dowry."

Edward rolled his eyes, condescension coloring his expression. "You are so naive. It's a good thing you have me to look out for you."

"Edward, what did you say to him?"

He blinked, likely taken aback by the hard edge to her words. "I told him I knew he was in straits and sniffing about for your dowry."

Daphne narrowed her eyes. "You have no idea

of what you speak."

Edward crossed to stand before her, still only an inch taller for all his nineteen years. "I do, Daph. It's all over London how our cousin found out his uncle is strapped and that Mr. Garrick was after her dowry, and that's why she had to throw him over."

"That is what's all over London?" *Poor Mr. Garrick. How would such terrible tales get spre—*

"Wendy," Daphne muttered in answer to her own silent question.

"Yes, our cousin, Wendy. You were there. You must already know what happened."

Daphne uncurled a hand to poke Edward in the chest. "Yes. I was there." She poked him again, causing him to take a half step back. "And as such, I believe you should give me credit for enough intelligence to know if the gentleman is after my dowry or not." She capped that with another jab.

"Ow." Edward rubbed his chest. "You don't even know what your dowry is, so how can you know if someone is after it or not?"

"I don't need to know." Her eyes narrowed. "How is it that you do? Father wouldn't have told you."

Edward flushed. "I, ah, happened to see it on some papers his attorney sent for him to sign."

"I see." Daphne shook her head. Servants standing about the entrance hall caught her eye. Well, the damage was done, so they may as well hear all… including the truth. "You should know that Mr. Garrick's uncle is not in any way strapped."

Edward continued to rub his chest. "He isn't?"

She shook her head. "He simply wrote to Mr. Garrick forbidding him to marry our cousin, on pain of losing his fortune."

"Garrick's uncle was going to cut him off if he married her?" Edward shook his head. "So he threw her over? She started those rumors to salvage her reputation, then." Edward grimaced. "Not noble, but what could our cousin do when the man has no honor?"

"Do you ever stop to learn the truth before giving voice to your thoughts?" Daphne demanded. "Mr. Garrick declared he would marry her regardless and they would live on the two hundred pounds a year that her dowry and his savings would earn."

"Two hundred pounds a year?" Edward grimaced. "He would have done that?"

"Not only would he have, he made the offer several times." Daphne swallowed as a sudden lump threatened to tinge her voice with tears. "For whatever reason, he's in love with her."

"So, she threw him over because she didn't want to be poor?"

"Exactly, and then she started a rumor so she wouldn't look like the fortune hunter she is."

"Oh." Edward looked down, abashed. "I, ah, owe Garrick an apology, then."

"Undoubtedly." If they ever saw the gentleman again. Poor Mr. Garrick. Already maligned by Wendy, he'd had to face Edward's ridiculous, unsubstantiated allegations. "It's a wonder he didn't challenge you."

Edward grimaced. "I'm sorry, Daph. I was only trying to look out for you, what with Father too busy with Irving to do it." Worried hazel eyes met her gaze. Edward swallowed audibly. "Do ah… do you think Irving is going to wake up?"

Daphne's anger froze and blew away, like snowflakes in the wind. "Yes. Certainly he will. I should get back to him. Mother took a break earlier. Perhaps I can persuade Father to as well."

Edward nodded. "Let me know if I can help."

She forwent a comment on that and brushed past him to climb the staircase, then hurried down the hall to her youngest brother's room. Pausing to gather quiet and calm about her, Daphne opened the door to the room.

"How is he?" she whispered, stepping inside.

Her parents looked up with blurry, tired eyes.

"No change," Mother said.

Daphne crossed to her father. "I'll stay with Mother and Irving. I can tell you've hardly slept since he fell."

Her father looked past her, to her mother, expression questioning.

"Go, Paul. Daphne and I will stay."

Wearily, he stood, then dropped a kiss on Daphne's brow. "Thank you. Let me know if there is any change."

Daphne nodded. She took his chair as he left the room, the door closing quietly behind him. Leaning forward, she collected Irving's hand, seated as she was beside his uninjured arm, and spoke a quiet prayer. When she opened her eyes, she found her mother watching her.

"It was very kind of Mr. Garrick to bring you here. Will he remain for the night?"

Daphne shook her head, annoyance sparking. "He will not. Edward drove him away because of some ridiculous rumor he heard in London."

Mother let out a heavy sigh, making Daphne wish she'd been less forthright. "What happened?"

Daphne worried her lower lip with her teeth, undesirous of adding to the tension lining her mother's features.

"It will be a good distraction," Mother said.

Like as not, that was true.

Daphne nodded and related the tale of Mr. Garrick's failed proposals and the rumor Cousin Wendy had surely begun. Her mother didn't interrupt, but did shake her head sadly, and even winced several times.

When Daphne finished, she met her mother's gaze squarely. "Now you tell me, what really happened between Father and Uncle Barlow?"

Her mother sighed. She reached out a hand to stroke Irving's hair, but her unfocused gaze rested somewhere across the room. "Your aunt and I were very close. Not twins, but only a year apart, like you and Edward, and both girls. We did everything together, including come out. We both met gentlemen. We had a joint wedding. Everything seemed perfect."

Silence fell.

"But it wasn't?" Daphne prompted after a

moment.

Mother shook her head. "Your uncle had a reputation. Your father, in contrast, was always studious and quiet. Your uncle took it into his head that he should show his new brother by marriage how to live. He took your father to numerous unsavory places and introduced him to the people one finds in them. He taught your father to gamble, to drink and to… Well, he introduced your father to a certain lifestyle and a different sort of women than one finds amongst the ton."

"The actress," Daphne guessed.

"Yes, the actress." Mother's tone held that same disdain as when she'd first mentioned the woman before Daphne had gone to visit her cousins. "Your father fell madly in love with her."

Daphne gasped. "But, you were already wed."

"We were."

"But…" Daphne trailed off. She would never have thought such a thing of her staid, devoted father. "What happened?"

"At first she enjoyed his devotion, especially the gifts." Mother said the word 'she' with the utmost disdain. "Later, she grew weary of him. She and your uncle thought it would be amusing to carry on an affair behind his back. He caught them and challenged your uncle. It was then that the woman admitted she'd never cared for your father and had already tired of him, but your father thought maintaining his challenge would win her love. Your uncle said he wasn't fool enough to risk his life for a… well, a woman who lacked moral character. The entire argument took place at their club. There were numerous witnesses. The whole sordid affair was the talk of London, with most people taking your father's side."

"Oh dear," Daphne breathed.

Mother nodded.

"Yet, you forgave him?"

To Daphne's surprise, her mother's cheeks pinkened.

"You see, dear, your father and I, despite being wed, had not... that is, we hadn't engaged in marital relations. To be honest, I was so relieved to discover the reason, I forgave him. All I asked was his devotion from then forward, and that we leave London. At the time, I made him promise we would never return, but that part of his vow seems silly now."

"So he came to love you?" Daphne held her breath, waiting for the answer.

"He did. He does. Very much, and I love him."

"And Aunt Barlow?" How had one couple grown stronger from the incident and the other been forced apart?

"For refusing your father's challenge, your uncle was branded a coward by the ton, for which he never forgave your father. Mary was already with child by then. Children, that is, as they are twins. I'm rather sure she achieved that state before they even wed." Her mother gave a sad shake of her head. "The incident brought to light not only the one affair but quite a few others in which your uncle engaged. Only, unlike your father, he refused to mend his ways. In punishment, I do not believe my sister ever performed a single wifely duty again. Eventually, they too retired to the country. Both to save money and for your uncle's health." Mother sighed. "I don't know all the details of those years, as your uncle forbade my sister from corresponding with me."

"And Mr. Garrick's uncle is one of those who decried Uncle Barlow and supported Father," Daphne concluded. How sad, to punish Wendy for the actions of her sire, and yet, they said the apple didn't fall far from the tree. Mr. Garrick's uncle must mean to protect him.

"Yes. They still correspond regularly. He and your father exchange investment advice."

"Who is Mr. Garrick?" a sleepy, boyish voice asked.

Daphne let out a gasp, her grip on her youngest brother's hand spasming.

"Irving," Mother cried in a low voice. She bent to kiss his cheeks.

"Eeew, Mom, stop it," he cried, trying to pull his hand away from Daphne. His eyes went wide. "Hey, why won't my arm move?"

"You fell from a tree, love," Mother said. "How do you feel?"

"Alright, I guess, but my leg hurts."

Daphne couldn't hold in a laugh, though the sound came out half as a sob. She hugged her brother's hand to her chest, a smile on her face that felt as if it might split her head in two.

Chapter Nine

Arthur alighted before his uncle's London home, then looked up and down the street, taking in the neat, if a touch small, homes. Miserable little townhouse indeed. Arthur crossed the walk to the wide granite steps. Edge of what was fashionable? He jogged up. Ridiculous. Perhaps a touch in need of repairs, but lovely all the same and in a perfectly respectable neighborhood. Had Edward Hayhurst even set eyes on the place before maligning it?

The door opened to reveal his uncle's aging butler, Charles, framed by a well lighted, modish entrance hall. Arthur strode in, offering a nod, and began stripping off his gloves. The only reason his uncle lived in a slightly smaller than fashionable home was his bachelorhood. Even so, the space had proved more than adequate for the rearing of Arthur and Lillian after their unexpected arrival. Arthur had never found the house small, or unfashionable.

"Thank you, Charles," he said, handing his outerwear to the butler.

"Your uncle asked me to send you to him when you arrived, sir."

Arthur fished a watch from his waistcoat. "He wouldn't prefer I make ready for dinner and speak with him during the meal?"

Charles shook his head. "He said, with alacrity,

sir."

"Very well, then. The purple parlor?"

"Yes, sir."

Arthur nodded and went to the back of the house. He found his uncle ensconced in his favorite armchair, a heavily embroidered robe sashed closed over trousers, a shirt, and a waistcoat that strained at the seams. He clasped a cigar in one hand, a glass of brandy resting on a small table beside the other. As usual, the thick plum colored curtains were drawn closed. Mingled candle and cigar smoke hung heavy in the air, the latter floating in wafting trails above Uncle Garrick's head.

Arthur entered with a bow. "Uncle."

"Arthur. Have a seat." Uncle Garrick gestured with his cigar, then took a sip of brandy as Arthur complied. "I have news for you, boy. I didn't mean what I wrote in that letter. It was a test. The girl failed, I imagine, but at least now you know the truth. So, now that you're to be rich again, do you still want her?"

Arthur gaped at him, glad he was already seated. "A test?"

Miss Hayhurst had been correct in that guess? Arthur conjured Wendy's resolute features. She was not going to be pleased that she'd been so manipulated.

"Yes." Uncle Garrick nodded, compressing his chins.

Arthur sat back, blinking. He could turn around. Go back to the Barlows' estate. He'd missed

Wendel and Wendy's birthday, but he would be forgiven.

Should he? Did he wish to? Wendy's rejection had cut, especially the final time he'd proposed.

Yet, the quickest way to refute the rumors she'd started would be to wed her, and then he could go on with his plans for Lillian's Season. His sister would have a guardian and advocate. Yes, Wendy had rejected him with all vehemence, but he'd asked her to give up much. Besides which, once they wed, her drive and passion would be focused on aiding him and Lillian. No one would make so formidable an advocate as Wendy Barlow.

On top of that, he might still love her. Certainly, where his visions for the future used to reside, a dull pain now lurked. Not as sharp as in those first moments of betrayal, but pain nonetheless. Sorrow for the death of a life to which he'd aspired.

"Well, boy? Going to run back to her?"

The underlayment of disdain in his uncle's tone alerted Arthur. He narrowed his gaze. "I'm not certain, sir. What do you think I should do?"

Uncle Garrick chuckled but shook his head. "Not quick enough, boy. I raised you and I can read your thoughts before you have them. That you even considered taking that Barlow hussy back is all the answer I require." He took another sip of brandy. "I'm afraid the time has come for you to learn a hard lesson."

Arthur grimaced. When it came to Uncle Garrick, Arthur never proved quick enough. The letter hadn't been a test, but truth. The real test had begun the moment he'd entered the room.

"What lesson?" he asked in resignation.

"Come September, you are leaving this house."

Arthur shook his head. "And going where?"

Uncle Garrick shrugged. "How should I know? Wherever your one hundred pounds a year will take you."

"You're tossing me out?"

"And cutting off your allowance."

"But, why?"

Uncle Garrick puffed on his cigar. "I can't trust you with my fortune."

"You mean, you really will leave everything to the church?" Arthur stared at his uncle in horror.

"I will. It's the only way to ensure that not a penny of mine will ever go to that girl. She is her father through and through."

Arthur shook his head. "The point is moot. She won't have me."

"She will if I die, boy. I'm not going to live forever. I can't even get up from this chair without calling a servant to help."

"What if I swear not to wed her?" Did Uncle Garrick wish to see him beg?

His uncle studied him a long moment. "No. I think not. The little vixen is too cunning."

"What if she weds?" Arthur asked, desperate. "Then you won't have to fear I'll marry her."

"Like as not, the moment I'm dead, her husband will be, too, and she'll be after you again."

"Wendy is not a murderer," Arthur snapped, some of his patience fleeing him. "You're being unreasonable."

"It's my fortune, boy. Created with Paul Hayhurst's help. Your little hussy's father would have seen Hayhurst's life ruined, simply for the amusement of it. My decision stands."

Dread snaked through Arthur. He'd never known his uncle to change his mind. Ever. "What about Lillian? She is to have a Season."

Uncle Garrick shrugged. "She is your ward now. Her schooling is paid up until the end of the summer. Then, you will have some difficult decisions to make. Do you delve into your principal to give your sister a proper home and a Season, hoping that she captures the eye of a wealthy man, or do you keep your money invested and attempt to live off the interest? You'll likely have to let your valet go, and her maid. Perhaps sell some of your possessions."

Arthur shook his head, numb. "But… I'm not going to marry Miss Barlow."

"I won't take that chance, boy." Uncle Garrick puffed at his cigar. "Buck up. It's only May. You have four months to plan."

Arthur could only stare at his uncle, unable to find words.

"You can always find an heiress to marry, boy. Turn the tables. A woman would have done the same to you."

"Will you at least hire a companion for Lillian?" Arthur asked. "She can hardly have a Season without a chaperone."

Uncle Garrick shook his head. "What happens

to your sister is up to you. You are her guardian. Now, go and change for dinner. I thought we'd eat in here tonight. I don't fit in any of the dining room chairs anymore. Having a new one made. It isn't ready yet."

Dinner? That's all his uncle could think about? Without funds, where would Arthur and Lillian go? How would he even retrieve her from finishing school?

"The carriage?"

"Mine," Uncle Garrick said. "But you may use it until September."

"My team? My stallion?"

"I'm afraid you'll find that my money paid for them all, but I will gift you the stallion. I've no use for a riding mount. Especially a frisky one."

Arthur grimaced. "What about my clothing?"

Uncle Garrick snorted. "I've also no use for your clothing. You're a head taller and a good six stones lighter."

Arthur scrubbed his hands over his face. "Is this another test?"

Finally, a hint of compassion touched Uncle Garrick's expression. "It is not. As I said, hard lessons, boy. Learn them."

"Everything to the church?" Arthur pressed again, unable to believe his uncle would do such a thing.

"If I become satisfied that you've learned your lessons, that you see that girl for the devil spawn she is, you will be welcomed back and your allowance and inheritance reinstated."

"And how do I convince you that I will never marry Miss Barlow?"

Uncle Garrick shrugged, the movement a ponderous ripple of his embroidered robe. "Marry someone else."

His uncle was mad. Arthur had spent years planning to marry Wendy. There was no one else.

"I suggest you cultivate some new friendships, boy. Not only to meet eligible women but also so you may impose on them. It's the trick of every pockets to let gentleman." His uncle frowned. "Or I suppose you could borrow."

Wonderful. He would end up in debtor's prison or become a hanger on. A leech. That was to what Uncle Garrick would reduce him. Arthur would rather leave. Take his interest for the year and buy a commission. Die on the Continent with honor. Except, what would happen to his sister?

"If I were… gone, then you would take Lillian in, wouldn't you?"

Uncle Garrick's expression hardened. "Because you ask that question, the answer is no."

Arthur narrowed his gaze at his uncle. He couldn't mean that. "She is your niece. You raised her from a child of three."

"I am an uncompromising man, Arthur. That is why I never wed." Uncle Garrick downed the remainder of his brandy. "Now go and ready for dinner. I wish to hear of your travels."

Arthur surged to his feet. "I've lost my appetite, sir. I believe I will retire early."

"As you wish."

Hands clenched at his sides, Arthur offered a bow. His legs couldn't move quickly enough as they carried him from the room. His only cogent thought was to ask, over and over: *What can I do?*

Chapter Ten

A sultry May in the countryside, Daphne discovered, meant an unbearable May in London, but as the next Season would begin early, due to the vote, so must their preparations. Daphne knew this, but the knowledge made London no more bearable. Even so early in the month, the streets and buildings of the city soaked in the heat. They held it and amplified it to radiate outward again at far greater strength. The river ran low and sluggish. The sky was a dusty, unappealing gray blue. As far as Daphne could tell, the only bearable point in the whole of London was the park. Yet, her mother had insisted they come, wishing to beat the autumn rush of young women and their chaperones, all clamoring for new gowns.

"Because you are first," the modiste had said around the mouthful of pins pinched between her lips as she adjusted Christine's hem, "You will set the fashion for the Season." She glanced up with avaricious eyes. "You did say three full new wardrobes?"

Daphne's mother had said that. New day dresses. New evening gowns. Afternoon dresses, walking dresses, riding habits, traveling dresses and dinner dresses. Bonnets and gloves. Cloaks, slippers, and boots. Chemise and stays. Spencer and pelisse and everything in between.

Daphne knew her parents were wealthy, but she'd never been witness to such excess. Her mother seemed equal parts entertained and harried. Christine shone daily with delight. And so it went, day after day, ever since their arrival, until Daphne simply could not countenance any more.

That afternoon, declining to accompany her mother and sister on an outing to select new ribbons to match the new gowns being made, Daphne chose instead to wander the walks of the park, her maid and a footman trailing behind. In the country, Daphne would have been permitted to walk alone, or with only a maid. In that case, she and the girl could have conversed. In London, Daphne walked ahead, silent, while her maid whispered with the footman, occasionally emitting a giggle.

She started around a hillock, veering away from the wider tracks where riders and carriages could be found. During the Season, according to her mother, the park brimmed every afternoon. Gentlemen and ladies walked and rode, showing off their finery and scrutinizing one another. Daphne supposed that would be quite the sight but couldn't help but prefer the park nearly empty. Nature should be a place to escape the pressures of society.

She approached a second hillock, aware from previous walks that, on the other side, a bridge arched over a wide stream. Daphne found a certain amount of peace there, the water still bubbling in May. She liked to watch it swirl endlessly away.

Sometimes, she would drop leaves in, to speed off. Today, she'd brought a crust of bread to entice the ducks.

She rounded the hill to the off-putting sight of someone on her intended bridge. A gentleman who leaned out over the water as she had planned to, folded arms braced on the railing. She started to turn away when the gentleman tipped his head back to stare up at the muddy-blue sky. Wavy black locks protruded from beneath his hat, his profile familiar.

"Mr. Garrick," she called, starting forward again. She'd never had the opportunity to thank him for returning her home at the end of April.

He turned, gray eyes revealing surprise, then executed a deep bow. "Miss Hayhurst. It's a pleasure to see you."

"And you, sir."

"And may I say you look lovely this afternoon?"

Daphne's cheeks heated. "I suppose you may, so long as I do not misconstrue."

His lips pulled into a grimace. "Never fear. I have been warned from pursuing you."

Daphne shook her head. "That is not what I meant. I meant only to show deference to your devotion to my cousin."

His expression of displeasure deepened. "I no longer carry such devotion."

"Oh," she said, acutely aware that the conversation did not progress well. She glanced about, seeking more words. Her maid and footman had stopped some paces away, out of earshot, under the shade of a maple.

Mr. Garrick shook his head. "I apologize. My grim mood is hardly your fault."

"Grim mood?" Did he still pine for Wendy, despite his declaration of a lack of devotion? "May I ask what troubles you?"

"You have not heard of my woes?"

Daphne shook her head. "We've spent nearly all our time ordering our wardrobes and being fitted. That is the purpose of this trip. We leave at the end of the month, not to return until late October."

"We?"

"My mother, me, and Christine."

"I see."

He turned back to the rail to once again rest his folded arms there. Daphne moved to his side and leaned out to gaze into the water. Silence settled between them. She wondered if she should ask again to hear his woes.

"I did not have the opportunity to make the acquaintance of Miss Christine when I visited your family's country seat," he said.

"You will know her at a glance. She is the image of my mother, whom you did meet." Daphne cast a quick look his way. He made a study of the slowly moving water. "And I did not have the chance to properly thank you for bringing me home, which I do."

"You are most welcome. Your younger brother is well, I hope? You do not wear black and your mother and sister are in town with you, so I have hope that he recovers."

Daphne smiled, as she always did when she thought on Irving's recovery. "He is well. His arm and leg are still splinted and he complains daily, but he woke from the knock to his head and seems to have suffered no ill effects from it."

The smile Mr. Garrick turned on her shone with genuine relief. "I am pleased to hear it. For his sake and all of yours."

His kindness encouraging her, she ventured, "I… I apologize for Edward. He spoke out of turn."

Mr. Garrick's smile disappeared. "Ah, so you have heard rumors."

"From Edward, yes, but I know they aren't true. Your uncle is not devoid of fortune and you were not after Cousin Wendy for her dowry. Do not forget, Mr. Garrick, I was present."

Gray eyes measured her. "I will never forget that you were present."

Unaccountably, her cheeks heated again. "I am sorry Edward believed tales about you."

Mr. Garrick shrugged. "The rumors perpetuated by your brother were an annoyance but caused me no great concern. Any who wish to ask may have the truth of that matter from me. Most will reason out that I did not throw over Miss Barlow, for Wendel has issued no challenge on his sister's behalf."

"Yet, you still seem troubled." Had more ill befallen Mr. Garrick?

He studied her again, with no indication that he intended to speak.

"I do not mean to pry, but I would care to know," Daphne pressed. "Perhaps there is some way in which I might help, to repay you for bringing me home?"

He pressed his lips into a hard line.

"Please, Mr. Garrick? Unless it is something inappropriate for my ears? I would like to assist you."

"It is not me," he finally said, "but Lillian I worry for."

"Your sister?"

He nodded. "You see, out of fear that I will still wed Miss Barlow, or that she might try to win me back and I will succumb to her wiles, my uncle has decided to write me out of his will. Then, come September, he means to discontinue my allowance and no longer permit Lillian and me to reside with him."

Daphne pressed a hand to her chest. That was worse than she'd imagined. "But, your sister is to come out this Season, is she not? Have you told her?"

He shook his head. "I keep trying to compose the letter, but I cannot bring myself to."

"Where will you go? How will you live?"

He angled his gaze away from her, looking out over the stream. "Ever since he told me, I've saved every penny. I've sold a few heirlooms. I... I don't want to have to let our servants go. This isn't their fault. If they'll come with us, we have a small cottage in the country, left to me by my parents. I'll have to evict the tenants. I need the home more than their rent, for it can't pay for rooms in town. Ones for me, perhaps, but not ones suitable for Lillian. I have no notion how I'll afford a companion for her, so she may make calls. I can escort her to some events, but others will require a female."

"Have you no acquaintances to whom to turn? No other relations?"

He shook his head. "Most of my companions are single young men, like myself. On top of that, with no funds and no inheritance, a truth Miss Barlow unhelpfully spread when she thought it a lie, I suddenly find that most of my friends are not."

"Even my cousins?"

"Wendel would be. Will be, I suppose, again, but not now. Not with all that passed between Miss Barlow and me."

Daphne worried her lower lip with her teeth, thinking. She truly ought to ask her parents first, but… "Miss Garrick could stay with us, and we could be her companions. Me, Mother and Christine. Then, you could rent rooms, and not have to evict your poor tenants or remove your servants and sister from London."

He whirled to face her. "You…you would take Lillian in?"

"Certainly." At least, so she hoped. The joy in his eyes set her heart hammering. "You helped me when I needed to return home."

"This is a greater favor. Especially—" He broke off with a frown. "You realize that there is a black mark beside my name now, which will also smudge my sister's. Consider that before you ally yourself, and Miss Christine, with us. I know you must both find husbands."

"We don't know anyone in London, anyhow. Besides which," she continued when he opened his mouth to speak, "I do not wish to make the acquaintance of anyone who would either believe my cousin's lies or shun you for your change in circumstance."

"You are very kind, Miss Hayhurst."

Somehow, Daphne had missed having those gray eyes on her. "It is not so large a favor as that."

"Even so, I believe you must discuss it with your family before I hold you to your offer."

"That is considerate, but I believe they will agree."

"Thank you." He captured her hand. "It was my good fortune to meet you on your walk today, Miss Hayhurst."

Daphne could only nod, not able to speak as he bowed over her hand. He did not, as she hoped, graze her knuckles with his lips. Of course, she wore gloves, as did he, so the experience wouldn't have been the same. Even so, heat stole into her cheeks.

"I ride out tomorrow to inspect the cottage," he said. "Perhaps when I return to London, I may call on you?"

"Call on me?" Did he mean… court her? "As I noted, we will remain until the end of May."

He nodded. "It is a journey of nearly a week each way, with at least one day spent in the inspection of the property, but I will be back before the month is out. When I return, if I may, I will call to seek your family's mind on your kind offer for Lillian's Season?"

Not to court her, then. She couldn't contain a tinge of disappointment. She mustered a nod. "Certainly. We will look forward to your visit."

"Thank you." He bowed again. "Enjoy your fittings, Miss Hayhurst."

"Have a safe journey, Mr. Garrick."

He nodded, then turned in the opposite direction from which she'd come. Daphne suppressed a sigh as she watched him walk away.

Chapter Eleven

Arthur descended the inn's staircase, rolling his shoulders to relieve the stiffness there. He'd left Stenson in London at his uncle's and ridden out alone, and this was his second night of sleeping in cramped, less than adequate beds. If Arthur had a touch less pride, he might have considered his uncle's suggestion that he hunt down an heiress to wed. Being short of funds was already proving even more miserable than he'd imagined.

The inn boasted private parlors, but Arthur made his way to the common room to partake of whatever fare with which general patrons broke their fast. Entering, he spotted a vase of wildflowers placed in a deep-set window, the blooms luminous with morning light. Unbidden, a vision of Miss Daphnc Hayhurst twirling about the valley floor brought a smile to his lips. Even more so than the flowers, she'd been luminous that morning. Nearly irresistible, despite his esteem for Wendy.

His smile broadened slightly as he recalled the kiss which he'd placed on the back of Miss Hayhurst's hand. She'd gasped, clearly surprised, but hadn't pulled away. Arthur had no idea what had driven him to such impropriety. With Wendy, he'd always been master of himself, no matter how extreme her flirtations. One pretend dance with

Miss Hayhurst and his restraint had scattered like so many falling petals. Shaking his head at such errant, nonsensical thoughts, he took a seat at the table nearest the flowers, enjoying the reminder of that stolen, carefree moment in the valley.

Miss Hayhurst often delighted him, he'd found. As with her touching concern for Lillian. She'd never even met his sister, yet she'd offered aid. He didn't hold much hope that her parents would overlook his current label of persona non grata to permit Lillian to reside with them, but Miss Hayhurst's heartfelt offer showed great kindness, nonetheless.

"Mr. Garrick?"

Arthur turned to see the innkeeper approaching at a rapid pace. "Yes?"

"Sir, this arrived for you in the middle of the night. The rider said it's urgent."

Arthur frowned, worry shooting through him. He'd only two relations, and only trouble with his relations could necessitate such hurry. He accepted the missive, noting his attorney's seal. Unsettled, Arthur cracked the message open. He skimmed the salutation to reach the heart of the matter.

Your uncle left us early this morning. You should know that he ordered his will to be changed only if you wed Miss Wendy Barlow. You remain his sole heir.

Arthur stared at the page. He blinked several times. Carefully, hands shaking slightly, he folded it closed, then sank back in his chair.

"Bad news, sir?" the innkeeper asked.

Arthur realized that the man still hovered nearby. "My uncle is dead."

"I'm sorry to hear that, sir."

Uncle Garrick had always been ill. Arthur had known he would one day be gone, just as his parents were. Inevitable, really. He simply had not expected it to happen anytime soon. He also hadn't expected… he cracked the missive open again.

You remain his sole heir.

How could three lines be simultaneously so painful and yet offer so much relief? Arthur fixed his gaze on a blank section of wall, unable to comprehend how he ought to feel.

One thing he did know, how Lillian would feel. She would be devastated. Would she receive a letter as well? Arthur couldn't let her find out from a letter, while away at school. Even if the attorney did not write, rumor would carry the news nearly as fast. Arthur surged to his feet and looked about, only to find that the innkeeper still hovered at his shoulder.

Extracting several large denomination notes from his cache of ready funds, Arthur pressed them on the innkeeper. "This should cover my stay. In addition, I require a carriage, as well as someone reliable to ride my mount back to London."

The innkeeper nodded. "My lad can take your horse, sir. He's right reliable, and I'll send for a carriage."

"Thank you. I'll be back down momentarily with my bag."

"I can send someone up to pack it for you, sir,

if you would care to break your fast?"

Arthur shook his head. "I didn't arrive with much."

He strode back through the common room and up the narrow staircase. In short order, he'd turned his stallion over to the innkeeper's son and climbed into a carriage. Having given directions before getting in, Arthur knocked on the roof to set them in motion.

As the carriage, serviceable but in no way as fine as even the meanest of Arthur's uncle's, rumbled down the dusty lane leading away from the inn, Arthur settled back in his seat. The carriage would be the first of several, for the trip would take days. Arthur grimaced. That would give him considerable time to think. A hard lump filled his throat. Several swallows did nothing to dislodge it. Arthur hadn't said farewell to Uncle Garrick when he'd left London to go inspect the cottage. Hadn't even waited for the older man to awaken that day. He'd considered the lack of courtesy his uncle's due for the torment he'd unleashed on both Arthur and Lillian, although he'd hoped to somehow keep Lillian from enduring most of it.

Now, it seemed more as if he'd stormed off, like a child. Like the angry, black haired cloud of bitterness he'd been when Uncle Garrick first took them in, all those years ago. Arthur closed his eyes. Only seven, his little sister a child of three in their nanny's arms, they'd arrived on Uncle Garrick's doorstep. Even then, some fourteen years ago, Uncle Garrick had walked with a cane. He'd looked them over, let out a thunderous sigh, and turned to lumber away. As if in afterthought, he'd glanced over his shoulder and told Charles to permit them inside.

The carriage thudded over a rut in the road, the springs definitely not up to Uncle Garrick's quality. Arthur forced his eyes open. He swiped a hand across each cheek, unsure when tears had fallen.

He cleared his throat and sat up straighter. Better to look to the future. There was naught he could do to fix the past.

They would need mourning clothes. Lillian would require a chaperone. The two of them couldn't simply live alone in… in Uncle Garrick's townhome. Not and properly receive callers, and callers there would be. Everyone who'd recently ignored Arthur in his moment of insolvency would reappear, full of condolence.

And Arthur would receive them. He would be polite. Courteous. Like as not, he wouldn't even tell Lillian about his interlude as a pauper. Society would continue to go around, and he and his sister must turn with it. At least, and especially until she found a husband. Arthur would do everything he could to mitigate any harm recent events had done to her chances.

A thank you for Daphne's offer was definitely in order, even if Arthur no longer required the assistance. Unfortunately, by Arthur's calculations, with the time he'd already traveled and the change in direction to collect Lillian, he was unlikely to return to London before the Hayhursts departed. He would be too busy making arrangements and too deep in mourning to call, regardless. He would simply have to write. He'd direct the letter to Mr. Hayhurst, as writing to any other member of his household would be improper. Should he address it to the gentleman's country seat or his London residence?

Country seat.

Arthur blinked several times. He had an estate now. One he'd never visited, as Uncle Garrick never left London. Arthur would need to learn about it. Their attorney would have ledgers, surely? Advice? Arthur rubbed his forehead. No matter what the attorney had, Arthur would need to go there to understand the running of the place. He would take Lillian, too. Their country manor would be a good place to observe mourning.

That decided, his mind wandered to his uncle again, conjuring memories. Thoughts in tumult, Arthur moved from sorrow to guilt, then anger, then back to sorrow. Much as he tried, he couldn't bring his musings, or emotions, into order. He continued to do battle as his rented carriage rumbled down the roadway.

Chapter Twelve

Daphne tugged back the carriage's curtain to watch their slow progress up the London street. She found the climate of the city much more bearable in November but felt the coolness offset by the mobs of people. Everywhere they went, London's elite bubbled forth, chatting and gawking. Ignoring and seeking not to be ignored. London society was nothing like her family's circle in the country.

At least inside the carriage they weren't crowded. Father's newest acquisition, bought for Daphne and Christine's Season, would easily hold six. Instead, only Daphne, her mother, Christine, and Edward rode within. Father had declined to attend the evening's festivities, saying that he preferred to dance in his own ballroom, and the four youngest Hayhursts had been left in the country, despite the girls' begging and Irving's protests that he could nearly walk normally again.

Christine, Edward, and their mother chatted amiably as they rode, but anxiety swirled through Daphne. This was their first ball in London. They'd only been in town for a few weeks. There had been, to her mother's considerable delight, a reunion with Aunt Barlow, with Wendel and Wendy conspicuously absent. They'd also taken a few teas, endured several trips back to the modiste and milliner, and received a handful of guests, but nothing had been on the scale of tonight's ball. Tonight, she and Christine would be on display for the bulk of the ton. Everything they did and said would be evaluated.

Christine appeared to feel no strain, but Daphne's greatest hope was to be so unremarkable as to be glossed over by her peers.

To that end, she wore a modest gown. Pale green, dotted with white and yellow flowers, and trimmed in an understated cream lace, it shouldn't garner a second glance from anyone. Unlike both Edward's and Christine's ensembles.

Christine wore a low-bodiced, slimly cut dress. The sky-blue material, several shades darker than a young woman supposedly ought to be clad in, matched her eyes to perfection. The gown was also trimmed in a stark white lace which somehow managed to make her curls appear even more golden than usual.

Daphne raised a hand to touch her carefully arranged curls. If she'd matched her clothing to her hair and eyes, she'd be wearing some combination of mud and dying leaves. That thought brought her attention to her brother, who had also inherited their father's middling brown tresses.

Unlike Daphne, who'd been required to wear a bonnet all summer to avoid freckles, Edward had managed to spend enough time out of doors that golden streaks shot through his hair. His eyes, not quite the blue of her mother's or sisters', were at least an appealing hazel. Not cat-yellow like Daphne's. To capitalize on that, he wore a mixture of bright blue and green, with orange and yellow embroidery thick on his coat and waistcoat. Daphne thought it rather much but, before they'd piled into the carriage, Edward had preened incessantly under the praise of the others.

They turned and Daphne peeked out the window again, but the angle of the drive allowed only a glimpse of the building, set back from the street. A familiar conveyance trundled by, empty and moving away from their destination. Daphne's anxiety vanished in a swirl of anticipation. The departing carriage, which appeared empty, belonged to Mr. Garrick.

She worked to tamp down rising excitement. Mr. Garrick had never given any indication that he preferred her company. Quite the opposite, really. Like the way he'd departed her family's country home without a farewell, or the note he'd sent her father. Not that Daphne had read the note, but her father had conveyed the content. Right after he'd asked her if she had promised that a young woman he'd never before met could reside with them.

Daphne hadn't yet worked up the exact way to ask her parents if Miss Garrick might spend the Season with them when the note arrived, making the question moot. She'd explained that to her father, any annoyance on his part mitigated by the lack of need. According to him, rather than calling on her as he'd said he would, Mr. Garrick had written to say that he had inherited his uncle's fortune and so could now procure a companion for his sister. In short, he no longer needed Daphne's help. Just like that, the connection she'd built with him had been sundered and, with her family returning to the country and him in mourning for his uncle, there'd been nothing for her to do about it.

Their vehicle came to a halt and the door opened. Daphne and her family climbed out. Daphne's gaze swept over the crowd of people entering the London townhouse. Tall and topped with wavy midnight locks, Mr. Garrick ought not to be difficult to find.

Yet she did not see him. She kept up her search as they climbed the steps, made their way through the entrance hall, and waited in the receiving line. She began to doubt that she'd correctly identified the carriage. They greeted their hosts, then entered the ballroom. Her mother, apparently too excited to maintain propriety, hurried off at the sight of an old acquaintance, leaving Daphne, Christine and Edward standing in the entryway.

The crowd shifted and Daphne spotted Mr. Garrick halfway across the room, impeccably clad in hunter green. Not the same coat he'd worn at the Barlows' home, for this one appeared new and much finer, though equally austere. As then, he wore a cream-colored waistcoat, also appearing new, over a pristine white shirt. His only adornment was an emerald which glinted against the white of his cravat.

"Who is that beauty beside Garrick?" Edward said in her ear.

Daphne blinked. She hadn't noticed the young

woman standing beside Mr. Garrick. Straight backed and tall, her slender build was nearly ethereal, an impression emphasized by tresses that mirrored Mr. Garrick's black and highlighted the paleness of her skin. She could only be his sister.

"She must be Miss Lillian Garrick," Daphne replied, voice quiet.

"Why is no one standing near them?" Christine asked.

"The new rumors," Edward replied.

Daphne turned to him. "What rumors? The ones Cousin Wendy spread about him being a fortune hunter?" Which were moot now that he'd inherited his uncle's fortune after all.

Edward shook his head. "There are worse ones now."

Daphne glanced again at Mr. Garrick and his sister. Christine was correct. Empty space ringed them, noticeable in the crowded ballroom. "Tell me."

Edward cast a quick look in the direction their mother had gone, then leaned close. Christine wiggled between them, expression curious, as Edward spoke in a low voice. "Now it's going around that Garrick murdered his uncle before the old man could change his will."

Christine gasped.

"That's ridiculous." Daphne shook her head. "Surely, no one believes such a tale?" Had their cousin started that rumor as well? No, Wendy wouldn't be that vindictive.

"Of course, no one believes it. He wasn't even

in London when it happened… although many of the rumors say it was poison and Garrick could have administered it before departing."

"Anyone who believes such a tale is daft," Daphne stated.

Edward shrugged. "As I said, no one really does."

"Then why isn't anyone speaking with them?" Christine asked.

"Well, first he was labeled a fortune hunter, then he began acting the pauper, selling things off and wearing old clothes. Now, everyone is whispering that he's a murderer. You have to admit, he looks rather grim with that frown and his black hair. Seems a bit evil."

"Edward, really." Daphne infused her words with condemnation.

Edward took a half step back, hands coming up as if to ward off her ire. "I didn't say that I believe any of it. I'm simply explaining."

Daphne squared her shoulders. "Well, I say we put an end to this all right now."

Christine caught her arm. "What are you going to do?"

"We are going over there so I may introduce you."

"Mother wouldn't want us to make a scene," Christine hissed, clutching Daphne's arm tighter.

"It is the right thing to do," Daphne said firmly. "Edward, Christine and I will start. You collect Mother."

"As my lady commands." Edward's tone held

good natured mocking. He executed a bow then hurried off.

"Must we?" Christine whispered as Daphne started across the ballroom.

"Yes. I believe we must."

If not because it was right, then because their cousin had caused much of Mr. Garrick's grief. As Wendy surely wouldn't make amends, Daphne felt obligated to.

Chapter Thirteen

A vision. That's what she was. The memory of whom, by dint of her simple kindness, had kept Arthur company throughout his months of mourning. And a vision who, gowned in pale green and topped with caramel curls above beguiling amber eyes, proved even more lovely in person than recollection. She brought her ostentatiously garbed younger brother with her, along with her mother and a stunning blonde, a younger version of that matriarch. Arthur bowed as they approached. Beside him, Lillian dropped a curtsy.

Arthur didn't need to force warmth into his tone as he greeted them. "Mrs. Hayhurst, Mr. Hayhurst, Miss Hayhurst. A pleasure to see you all again. May I present my sister, Miss Lillian Garrick."

Edward Hayhurst stepped forward to bow over Lillian's hand. "Miss Garrick, we're honored."

"Thank you, sir," Lillian murmured.

Arthur heard the relief in her tone. Lillian had grown increasingly nervous at their ostracization. It had pained him to see his little sister at her first ball, hope being replaced by confusion as no one approached.

"Miss Garrick," Mrs. Hayhurst greeted. "How lovely to make your acquaintance. I do not believe either of you know my second eldest daughter, Christine?" Mrs. Hayhurst smiled at Lillian. "I think the two of you to be of an age."

Arthur and Lillian greeted Daphne's younger sister, Miss Christine's reply proper but her tone lukewarm. Of all the Hayhursts, she alone appeared less than pleased to see them. Guessing by her bright gown and display of décolletage, Miss Christine was a young woman who intended to make somewhat of a spectacle of herself that Season. He could only hope, for Daphne's sake, not too great a one.

"Has anyone claimed the next set yet, Miss Garrick?" Edward Hayhurst asked.

Lillian's cheeks tinged pink. "No, Mr. Hayhurst. Not as of yet."

"Well then, I would be honored if you would stand up with me."

Lillian cast Arthur a quick, questioning look, to which he nodded his assent. She turned back to Hayhurst. "That would be pleasant. Thank you."

Hayhurst grinned like a schoolboy.

Arthur wondered if he should stand out so he could best watch over his sister. Yet, he'd often wondered what it would be like to dance a real dance with Daphne, not a stolen one in a meadow. Deciding Lillian was safe enough with Hayhurst, Arthur offered Daphne a half bow. "And I would be honored if you would dance with me, Miss Hayhurst, and then you, Miss Christine."

"Thank you," Daphne said.

Was that genuine happiness in her voice? It pleased Arthur to think so. They fell into talk of the weather while they waited for the start of the next set. The ring of empty space about them closed. The Hayhursts, with their wealth and what Arthur had come to understand was a sterling reputation, carried weight among the ton. More so than Arthur could, with his few connections.

He watched Daphne converse with her family and his sister, enamored with the ease of her, the openness in her expressions. She did not tease or taunt, flirt, or work to beguile. How different she was from her cousin. It chagrined him to have previously allied himself so strongly to the Barlows. To have believed their lies about Daphne and her family. For once, Arthur should have sought gossip and listened to it.

He suppressed a grimace. Gossip. His bane of late. Wendy would not stop spreading lies, each more absurd than the previous. Apparently, members of London society would believe anything if they heard it repeated often enough.

"And what have we here?" a slightly strained, familiar male voice said.

Arthur turned to find Wendel beside him. "Barlow," he greeted, unable to contain his surprise.

"Garrick, Cousin Daphne, I do not believe I know your friends." Wendel met Arthur's eyes, his own putting Arthur in mind of a puppy worried that it was about to be kicked.

Mrs. Hayhurst held out a hand to Wendel, her expression kind. "But you must, Nephew. I am your Aunt Hayhurst, and these are your cousins, Edward and Christine."

The pair nodded in turn.

Their mother shook her head. "For how many years have I longed to make your acquaintance? And now here you are at last."

Wendel darted an assessing look at Arthur, who kept his expression neutral, before stepping forward to bow. "I must believe you have waited for one and twenty years, as have I. Aunt, Cousins, it brings me great happiness to finally meet you. Aunt Hayhurst, you are the very image of my mother."

"Your mother said you and your sister would arrive in town today," Mrs. Hayhurst said. "I assume they are here with you?"

As well as Arthur knew him, he could see the tension in Wendel. Read it on his face and in his voice, in the way that Wendel kept darting looks his way as if Arthur might bite.

"Yes, Wendy and I arrived today. Mother, sadly, is indisposed this evening and Wendy did not feel that she had enough time to prepare for a ball." Wendel essayed a grin. "I do not require quite so much primping."

Edward Hayhurst snorted. "Aye, you should have seen the fuss where we reside. Christine was in a tizzy nearly the entire day."

"As were you, Edward," Christine retorted. "Anyone can see you're a dandy."

Edward Hayhurst narrowed his eyes.

Arthur took in the resigned look that flitted across Daphne's face. Did her siblings often disagree, then?

As if also sensing an impending argument, Wendel whirled to face Lillian. "I also do not believe I know this young lady."

"You do, Mr. Barlow," Lillian said. "We've met on more than one occasion."

Wendel's eyes flew wide in surprise. "Miss Garrick?" He shot Arthur a startled look. "When did you grow into a young lady? The last I saw you, you were... that is..."

Arthur frowned. He didn't care for the way Wendel looked Lillian up and down. He wasn't even certain he cared for Wendel's company in any form. Not with Wendy spreading malicious gossip about him. "You would see her more often were your sister and I not at odds."

Wendel grimaced. "Look, Garrick, I'm sorry about that. I swear to you, I tell the truth as often as I can." He shrugged. "Many people simply prefer lies. They make better stories."

"What lies?" Lillian asked, eyes wide.

Silence descended on their small group. Around them, the room buzzed with conversation and music.

"Arthur?" Lillian aimed a confused expression at him.

Beside her, Wendel looked strained.

"Perhaps that is something for a later discussion?" Mrs. Hayhurst suggested. "Now, it is time to enjoy the ball."

Lillian looked at her, then nodded. Daphne and her sister watched the exchange with wide eyes, Daphne's showing concern and Miss Christine's avid interest.

"I believe that the next set is about to begin," Edward Hayhurst said with forced cheer. He stepped to Lillian's side. "Our promised dance."

Lillian gave him a tentative smile. "Yes. I think you are correct."

"And may I have the following set, Miss Garrick?" Wendel asked.

She turned back to him with pursed lips. "I once attempted to practice dancing with you, sir. You laughed and told me to return to playing with my dolls."

Arthur bit back a laugh. Wendel deserved his sister's wry comment.

"He did not," Miss Christine gasped. "Cousin, how terrible."

Wendel grimaced, expression abashed. "I would also like to claim a set from you, Cousin Christine, and you, Daphne."

Miss Christine tipped her nose into the air. "I will see how you dance with Miss Garrick. If you know the steps well enough, then I will dance with you."

Wendel's eyebrows shot up.

Arthur stifled another chuckle.

Edward Hayhurst offered his arm to Lillian. "Our set?"

She proffered a white-gloved hand. Hayhurst placed it on his sleeve and led her to where other couples assembled.

"Miss Hayhurst?" Arthur asked. "If you will excuse us, Mrs. Hayhurst."

"That leaves you with me, Cousin," Wendel said behind them as Arthur led Daphne away. "On my honor, I know the steps at least as well as Garrick there."

Miss Christine let out a lugubrious sigh. "I suppose we can try."

Arthur escorted Daphne to their place.

The musicians struck up a lively country dance, one Arthur knew well. The dance was quite similar to the reel he'd caught Daphne practicing, and she proved as lively and skilled in a ballroom as a meadow. That was fortunate, as the second dance in their set was equally energetic.

For the third dance, the musicians struck up a minuet, likely to permit the dancers to catch their breaths. Arthur captured Daphne's hand in his. He took in her pink-tinged cheeks. Exertion, or the effect of his presence? Unbidden, a vision of her bathed in sunlight and surrounded by wildflowers filled his senses.

"You and my cousin maintain your friendship?" she asked in a low voice as they walked slowly through a turn.

They switched hands and went back the other way, affording Arthur the view Daphne must have had, of Wendel dancing with Miss Christine, their conversation appearing quite animated.

"This is the first I have seen him since I escorted you home in April."

"Half a year."

"For those six months, we were in mourning. At least my uncle was kind enough to stipulate in his will that the mourning be only six months, not a year. That has allowed Lillian to still have her Season."

Not that Arthur would have made any effort to seek out Wendel, were he not in mourning. To his way of thinking, Wendel must renew their friendship. Arthur and Daphne switched hands again, dipped, and turned. He could all but smell the scent of flowers wafting about them.

"My father informed me of your uncle's passing. My condolences on your loss."

Her quiet words, suffused with genuine feeling, reawakened the pain of his uncle's death. Arthur cleared his throat. "Thank you."

"I am also sorry for the way our cousin torments you."

"I think now, you do not mean Mr. Barlow."

Daphne shook her head. "I mean Wendy."

Arthur shrugged. "It is her way. She is a creature of passions."

Daphne's expression clouded. "Even now, you defend her?"

Did she wish to know if he still harbored affection for her cousin? "I comprehend her. That does not mean that I condone her actions." He essayed a smile. "But we should not permit her to tarnish our dance."

Daphne nodded. "Your sister is quite lovely," she offered in a change of topic. "I do believe my mother is correct that she and Christine are of an age."

Arthur darted a glance to where Lillian danced

with Edward Hayhurst. His sister wore a pleasant expression. They appeared to converse amiably. "She is nearly eighteen."

"Christine turned seventeen this March."

"Perhaps they will be friends. Lillian and her companion, Mrs. Smith, could call on you and your sister."

Daphne nodded. "I would like that."

Arthur gave her hand a gentle squeeze to convey his gratitude. They danced on, gazes locked. He could not determine if he breathed more freely in Daphne's presence, or if his chest constricted with longing. Both seemed equally true. He studied those beguiling amber eyes, wondering if she felt joy and longing in his presence, too. Did he dare attempt to find out? His heart thudded in his chest, the organ rather battered of late.

They entered into the final turn, which culminated in a bow. Arthur longed to peel back Daphne's glove. To caress skin that he knew to be silken smooth. To express his growing admiration through the touch of his lips.

Instead, he bowed a second time. "Thank you, Miss Hayhurst, for coming to our rescue tonight. I'd hoped to find that the rumors about me wouldn't hamper my sister's chances."

"Hopefully it makes up, in some small way, for the trouble my relations cause you."

"I do not hold you responsible for Miss Barlow's actions."

"Nor do I hold myself responsible. Still, it is right to make amends where we can."

"Thank you," he repeated, unable to read anything more than kindness in her response, and led her back to her mother.

Arthur did his duty by dancing with Miss Christine, who flirted nearly as well as Wendy, and then standing up with his sister. By then, the ring of uncertainty that had surrounded them had melted entirely away, and more gentlemen approached seeking introductions. Soon Daphne, Miss Christine and Lillian were encircled by a sea of potential suitors. With no reason to keep his sister from dancing and unable to enjoy standing up with other women when he knew that Daphne danced with other men, Arthur realized it would be a long time before he truly took pleasure in a ball.

Chapter Fourteen

Having finished her turn at the pianoforte, Daphne made her way across the room to where her sister and Miss Garrick stood beside an oversized Grecian column. As she'd played, Daphne had sighted them chatting and giggling, and felt a twinge of envy. Though they'd moved deep into November, attending parties, teas, balls, and various other outings, she'd yet to strike any true friendships, as it seemed Christine and Miss Garrick had.

"What are you two whispering about?" Daphne asked cheerfully.

Miss Garrick turned impossibly wide gray eyes on her. "Men."

"Shh, don't tell her. She's stodgy," Christine said with another giggle.

"I am not stodgy. What were you saying?" Daphne lowered her voice. "Is it about one of the men here?"

Blonde and black curls bounced as they shook their heads.

"Both of us are in love," Miss Garrick advised.

Daphne's eyebrows shot up. She believed that of Christine who, though she seemed to be enjoying her Season, still stubbornly adhered to her desire to marry Mr. Quincy, but could it also be true of Miss Garrick? She'd been away at school for the past several years. In the few weeks she'd been in London, she couldn't have spent much time with any specific gentleman. To the best of Daphne's knowledge, the only gentlemen who had danced with Miss Garrick at more than one event were Mr. Garrick and Edward.

"Who has captured your hearts?" Daphne asked.

They exchanged a look.

Christine turned back with a shrug. "We haven't decided if we should admit names yet."

Daphne narrowed her gaze. It wasn't often she got the chance to tease her sister. "I know who Christine esteems."

"Who is it?" Miss Garrick asked.

"I forbid you to say it," Christine cut in. "Not until Miss Garrick admits the name of her love."

Daphne raised an eyebrow. "Forbid me? Do you forget that I am your older sister?"

Wide gray eyes pleaded with Daphne. "Just a hint."

"Daph, don't."

"Tell me his initials, at least."

Much as she wished to gain Miss Garrick's esteem, Daphne relented and shook her head. "I'm sorry. If Christine doesn't want me to, I can't."

Christine let out a relieved sigh.

"I can."

All three of them whirled.

Wendy stepped around the column.

"Wendy," Miss Garrick cried, a smile wide on her face. She rushed to their cousin and held out her hands.

Wendy clasped them. She held Miss Garrick away from her. "What a lovely woman you've grown into, my dear."

"I haven't seen you in so long and now Arthur says he isn't to marry you but he won't tell me why. Whatever happened?"

Wendy turned artfully surprised eyes on Daphne. "You mean, Cousin Daphne has not told you yet?"

"Gossiping is a disagreeable, nefarious pastime," Daphne said, although she had the sudden suspicion that she was about to wish she'd engaged in it.

"I could not agree more," Wendy replied. "Which is why I'm so glad to be able to tell you the truth myself, Miss Garrick, but first, who is your lovely friend?"

Christine, who'd been eyeing Cousin Wendy with suspicion, stood a bit straighter at the compliment. "I'm your cousin, Christine Hayhurst."

"Why, I'd no idea I have such a pretty cousin. I must say, you and your sister look nothing alike."

Daphne narrowed her gaze, certain Wendy meant to insult.

Christine appeared pleased by the praise but tipped her head to the side. "Why did you say you could tell Miss Garrick the name of my beau?"

"Because I've heard all about your infatuation with Mr. Quincy. During her visit with us, your sister spoke of it as common knowledge."

Christine whirled to glare at Daphne. "Daph, how could you. Didn't you just say that gossip is disagreeable and nefarious?"

"Why yes, she did." Wendy turned around, thoughtful eyes on Daphne. "In fact, I feel ashamed to have spoken, Cousin Christine. I would never have uttered Mr. Quincy's name if I'd realized it was gossip."

"If you don't gossip, how do you even know?" Daphne asked. "I never told you. Only your mother."

"I believe, actually, that you told my mother and Mr. Garrick, while several of the staff listened. It's spoken of as common knowledge in our household. I don't recall anyone making mention of it being a secret."

"Daphne," Christine wailed, causing several nearby matrons to look their way, Miss Garrick's chaperone, Mrs. Smith, among them.

"Calmness, dear cousin, is essential," Wendy said. "You don't wish to cause a scene. No matter how badly betrayed you feel."

Christine leveled a glare at Daphne, lips pressed closed.

Daphne opened her mouth, then closed it again. She hadn't labeled the information as secret. It hadn't occurred to her that she might need to. Christine's infatuation had seemed a harmless enough topic. Finally, under the weight of her sister's glare, she ventured, "I… I didn't know it was a secret from our aunt."

"And Miss Garrick's brother?" Wendy said

sweetly.

"I can't believe you told everyone," Christine hissed at Daphne.

Miss Garrick's lovely gray eyes darted, taking them all in. "I'm certain that your sister meant no harm, and I shan't tell a soul." She turned a forcedly bright smile on Wendy. "You were going to explain what the trouble is between you and Arthur."

Wendy's expression crumpled. She let out a long, sad sigh. "I'm afraid it's all my fault. I fell into one of my tempers." She leaned close. "You see, I pleaded with your brother to kiss me. A single kiss, to seal our love. He would not. I admit I became angry. I refused him to punish him." She squeezed her eyes shut. A tear leaked from each. She opened them and dashed the tears away. "Now, I'm afraid it's gone too far. I'm afraid I've lost him forever."

Daphne frowned. She'd seen Cousin Wendy in a fit of passion. Her sorrow rang hollow by comparison.

Wendy placed a hand on Miss Garrick's arm. "Please, Lillian, will you help me win him back? May I call on you, at least, in the hope of encountering him?"

Christine shot Daphne another angry look and turned to Wendy. "Oh, you poor thing. Miss Garrick, you must let her call on you."

"Yes, certainly. I've been very sad to lose you as a sister."

A glint of triumph sparked in Wendy's blue

eyes, quickly supplanted by an overdone expression of hope. She clasped her hands to her breast, prayerlike. "Oh, thank you so much. With you as my ally, I cannot help but prevail upon his heart."

Daphne pursed her lips. She felt as if she should warn Mr. Garrick, or Miss Garrick.

"When should I call?" Wendy asked.

Miss Garrick opened her mouth, but Christine stopped her with a hand on her arm.

"Don't answer with Daphne here," her sister said, shooting Daphne a glare. "She'll warn your brother so he can avoid Cousin Wendy."

Three pairs of eyes turned to her.

Miss Garrick blinked rapidly, her expression touched with hurt. "Will you do that, Miss Hayhurst?"

Daphne hesitated.

"See?" Christine's expression revealed disdain. "She will. She'll get all sanctimonious about warning him, but really she'll be gossiping."

Daphne swallowed down hurt.

Miss Garrick's expression remained uncertain, but Wendy's was smug. Couldn't they see that she manipulated them?

"What about the rumors?" Daphne asked, seeing a way to prove Wendy's falsehood.

"What rumors?" Miss Garrick asked.

Eager to reveal Wendy's evil, Daphne let words rush out. "Cousin Wendy started terrible rumors about your brother. That's why no one would speak to you when the Season began."

Conflict registered on her sister's face, for surely Christine viewed the rumors as evil, too.

Miss Garrick's mien radiated confusion as she turned to Wendy. "Did you?"

Wendy shook her head. "I assure you, I did not." She grimaced. "I did write to some school friends explaining to them what had happened. I'm afraid they took it upon themselves to avenge me. I fear they began the rumors, but now I've begged them to stop."

"And… you'll refute the rumors?" Miss Garrick asked. "To everyone?"

Wendy nodded, her expression eager. "Certainly. Why would I not? I wish to wed Arthur and be your sister."

Christine touched Miss Garrick's arm again. She nodded her head away from Daphne and Wendy. The two younger women turned, blonde and raven haired heads together, as they whispered, leaving Daphne standing beside her cousin.

"You cannot hope to beat me at this game," Wendy said, voice very low. "I've spent years learning how to play."

"This is not a game. These are people's lives."

Wendy rolled her eyes. "So virtuous." She lowered her voice even further, her words sharp and hard. "Not only is it a game, it's the most important game that we play, and I will not lose, Daphne. Keep your person and your disgustingly sweet goodness away from Arthur and Lillian, or I promise you will pay."

Daphne stared at her, stunned by the raw hatred

in her cousin's voice. Wendy's expression morphed into a look of sweet, innocent eagerness. Daphne looked to find Christine and Miss Garrick turning back their way.

Christine stepped forward. "We would like you to go away, Daphne."

"I beg your pardon?"

"We considered taking Cousin Wendy and going somewhere else to speak but there are three of us and only one of you. We would appreciate it if you would go and stand somewhere else."

Daphne stared at her sister, hurt welling so fast that she had to blink back tears.

"Don't make a scene, Cousin," Wendy said. "It would pain us to see you embarrassed further."

Miss Garrick offered an apologetic grimace.

"Really?" Daphne blurted.

All three women nodded.

Blinking rapidly, Daphne turned and set out across the room. The lump in her throat only grew as she walked away.

Chapter Fifteen

"I don't see why Mrs. Smith cannot receive calls with you this afternoon," Arthur said, not for the first time. "It is the very purpose for which I hired her."

"I told you, I sent her to the shops for me," Lillian replied serenely.

Arthur drummed his fingers on the arm of his chair. They sat in the front parlor, not the back one his uncle had used. Arthur never went into that room, with its dark purple walls and permeation of cigar smoke. Though they'd mourned the proper six months the world expected for an uncle, Arthur still couldn't shake his sorrow for Uncle Garrick's passing or his guilt for the poor terms on which they'd parted. It seemed wrong to change his uncle's favorite room, yet Arthur held no interest in being there.

Charles entered and offered a bow. "Mr. and Miss Barlow are asking if you are at home."

"We are," Lillian said quickly before Arthur could reply.

Charles turned a questioning expression on Arthur.

"Please, Arthur?" Lillian asked.

He studied his sister through narrowed eyes. So, she plotted, did she? To what end? Perhaps he should be franker with her about why he and

Wendy were no longer on good terms. He'd sought to shelter Lillian from harsh truths about a woman she'd once thought would be her sister, but he would be more straightforward if that kindness forced him to endure Wendy's machinations.

"They are our friends," Lillian said quietly.

"Show them in, Charles."

Charles offered the slightest frown and bowed his way from the parlor.

"You cannot trust Miss Barlow," Arthur said to his sister, voice low.

"You don't understand. She's not to blame. You can't believe everything Miss Hayhurst says about her."

Arthur's eyebrows shot up. What had Daphne to do with it? Before he could frame the question, Wendel and Wendy entered. Arthur stood to greet them.

Wendel exuded happiness, his return greeting over eager. Arthur felt a touch of guilt for not speaking with his friend since their meeting at the ball. As much as Arthur was certain of Wendy's culpability in the rumors circulating about him, he felt equally sure of Wendel's innocence.

Wendy dropped into a deep curtsy, dipping forward to display her assets to full effect. As she rose, she met his gaze through long lashes. "Thank you for agreeing to see us, Mr. Garrick. I've longed for an opportunity to make amends."

Arthur imagined so, now that he'd secured his uncle's fortune.

"Should... shall we sit?" Lillian asked

tentatively. "I could send for tea?"

Wendy turned a charming smile on Arthur's sister. A pang assailed him for what a fine ally and advocate she would have been, for him and Lillian. At least, until they displeased her in some way.

"Actually," Wendy said, "I seem to recall that your library boasts an amazing atlas." She fluttered her lashes at Arthur. "I've longed to consult it again."

"Planning a trip?" Wendel asked.

Wendy issued a tittering laugh. "Certainly not. I simply enjoy learning about the world. I hoped Mr. Garrick could help me find the atlas so I could expand my knowledge."

Wendel snorted. "If that's what you want to call it."

Arthur eyed Wendy with disdain. "I'm afraid I've no notion where to find it."

"No?" Wendy winged an eyebrow upward. "Are you certain? We could search together."

"I'm certain."

Wendy turned a heartbroken look on Lillian.

Arthur ground his teeth together.

"I can find it," Lillian blurted. She glanced at Wendel. "I cannot carry it, though. It's, um, a very big book. You'd best come with me, Mr. Barlow."

"Right."

Wendel shot Arthur an apologetic look and proffered his arm to Lillian. The two of them fled into the hallway.

Arthur crossed the room and pulled the bellpull to ring for a servant.

"What are you doing?" Wendy asked.

"Calling a maid. It's not proper for us to be alone." Even with the parlor door open, he didn't trust Wendy.

She let out a sigh. "Don't be tiresome, Arthur."

"Tiresome? It's your reputation I guard." As well as his freedom. "And you should address me as Mr. Garrick, Miss Barlow."

Wendy moved to stand before him. She rested a slender hand on his chest. "Arthur, I'm sorry. I was foolish and upset. Of course I wish to marry you." Impossibly blue eyes gazed up at him. "I love you. I've loved you since the moment I saw you."

A shiver went through him, half fear, half desire. He'd dreamed of taking Wendy Barlow in his arms for years. Of possessing those lush curves. Being the focus of that indomitable spirit.

Except, the only true focus Wendy had was herself.

"As I recall, you disliked me the moment you saw me. You only came to admire me once you discovered I would inherit my uncle's fortune."

"Is it wrong for a woman to withhold her heart until she may discover if a gentleman can provide for her? Would you not think me foolish if I gave my admiration to a man who cannot keep me?" The hand on his chest stroked downward. "You, with your raven colored hair, your perfect features and broad shoulders, you're a danger to any woman." Her hand stroked back up. "The type of man who can capture a heart so thoroughly, no room for practical considerations remains."

Arthur captured her hand instead. Holding it in place, he took a step back. "Except that, with you Miss Barlow, only practical considerations ever remain."

Wendy frowned. "What are you saying, Arthur?"

"It's Mr. Garrick," he said firmly and released her hand.

A maid entered the room. "Sir?"

"Please select a chair and seat yourself," Arthur advised her. "Miss Barlow and I require a chaperone."

The girl's eyes went wide. "Y-yes, sir," she stammered and slipped into a chair along the far wall.

"Be reasonable," Wendy said, voice low.

"I believe that, in not casting you from my home, I am."

For a brief moment, a frown marred Wendy's face before she schooled her features into a pleasant expression. "Consider how good we are together. You are handsome and wealthy. I am beautiful, ambitious, socially adept. Together, we will be the most sought-after couple in London." Her eyes took on an avaricious glint. "Who knows? We could become companions to members of the peerage. Perhaps even royalty."

Arthur realized that, once, he'd thought such things mattered. "Yes, but could we be happy?"

"Social success will make us happy."

"It will make you happy."

Wendy's eyes narrowed. She drew in a hissing

breath. "You've found someone else."

He shook his head. "No. I've simply seen the truth of you."

Wendy whirled, paced away, turned back. "It's that Hayhurst chit, isn't it?"

"I beg your pardon?"

"How dare you replace me with my insipid, pathetic—"

"Guard your tongue Miss Barlow."

Her eyes flashed. "So it's true."

"I have no relationship with Miss Hayhurst, but your view of her can only serve to recommend her."

Wendy stormed up to him. A finger jabbed his chest. "My father knew how vile the Hayhursts are. That's why he drove them from London, despite the little thanks he got. Mark my words, if you do not resume your courtship of me, I will do the same."

Arthur shook his head. "Don't be absurd." He reached for the bellpull again. "I believe, Miss Barlow, the time has come for your brother to escort you home."

"You'll regret this, Mr. Garrick."

Arthur didn't bother to hide his disdain. "You're familiar with the location of the entrance hall. I'll direct your brother to meet you there." He walked past her but paused before leaving the room. "And, Miss Barlow? Keep your distance from my sister."

Ignoring Wendy's sputter of anger, Arthur left the room, but a finger of dread snaked through him.

He didn't know how, but he did know that Wendy would find a way to punish Daphne if she found her suspicion about his affections justified. As nothing actually existed between them, for Miss Hayhurst's own good, oughtn't he stay away?

Chapter Sixteen

Wrap in hand, Daphne knocked on Christine's door and entered.

Her sister looked up from her desk with a frown. She blew on the page before her, then folded it. "You do know that most people wait after they knock?"

Daphne halted her stride. She blinked twice, digesting the edge in Christine's tone, then proffered the wrap. "I'm sorry. You asked for this for your walk. As Cousin Wendy is to arrive soon, I thought there was a need to hurry."

Christine stood, shoving the folded page into her skirt pocket. "Oh, yes, I did. Thank you," she said as she came across the room. "You were correct. The color matches the embroidery on this gown to perfection."

She plucked the wrap from Daphne's hand and turned to the large mirror that stood beside her dressing table.

Watching her sister preen, Daphne adopted as casual a tone as she could muster. "To whom were you writing?"

"Hm?" Christine fluffed her curls above the wrap.

"When I came in, you were finishing a letter. Didn't you write to our sisters yesterday?" Justina and Katherine expected letters. Franklin and Irving did not, but maybe Christine had—

"Oh, that." Christine's tone held suspicious lightness. She continued to adjust her hair, not meeting Daphne's eyes. "It's only a note to Miss Garrick. Cousin Wendy will see her later. Saves the trouble of posting it."

Still suspicious but unwilling to alienate her increasingly prickly younger sister, all Daphne could think to say was, "Oh."

In the two weeks since Christine had met their cousin, she, Wendy, and Miss Garrick had grown rapidly close. Daphne wished she could be pleased, but she trusted Wendy not at all. Her interest in Miss Garrick seemed readily apparent. Wendy wished to ingratiate herself and win back Mr. Garrick. What Daphne couldn't deduce was what advantage Christine offered Wendy.

Christine finally turned from the mirror. Though lovely, with her golden curls and light blue gown, Daphne's darker blue wrap about her shoulders, her eyes held a touch of resignation. "Look, I know you and Cousin Wendy did not get on well when you visited and I know that you still dislike her on Mr. Garrick's behalf, but she is our cousin and he is, well, nothing to us."

An odd hollowness filled Daphne's gut at the truth of that. She'd only met Mr. Garrick that April. He'd known their cousins for years. Perhaps if his uncle hadn't passed and Miss Garrick truly had come to reside with them for the Season, they could have formed a bond. As it was, she saw him only on rare occasions.

Daphne tried to force a natural tone as she asked, "Do you believe he will forgive Wendy?"

Christine shrugged. "She did what she did out of passion, and passion is love. Lillian already forgave her."

How casually her sister mentioned Miss Garrick. Daphne knew that Mr. Garrick loved his sister. If only Daphne could have forged such a connection with her.

A maid stepped into the open doorway. "Miss Christine, Miss Barlow has arrived."

"Thank you," Christine said, then turned back to Daphne. "Will you come down to greet our cousin?"

Daphne shook her head. Part of her haste in bringing Christine the wrap was to avoid delivering the item in Wendy's presence. "I'm on my way to the library to practice my Italian."

Relief flashed in Christine's eyes. "I'll give her your regards, then."

Daphne nodded. They left the room, Christine closing the door behind her, and went in opposite directions. As she strode to the library, Daphne tried to tamp down her worry. Maybe Wendy's explanation for her treatment of Mr. Garrick was true. Maybe she did love him, not his fortune, and genuinely cared for Christine.

"E forse il sole non sorgerà domani," she muttered as she entered the library.

"Why wouldn't the sun rise tomorrow?" Edward asked, looking up from a book.

"I'm practicing my Italian." Daphne crossed to

sit opposite him.

He pointed a finger at her. "You look perturbed, sister dear."

Daphne worried her lower lip with her teeth. Finally, she nodded. "I am. Cousin Wendy is spending a great deal of time with Christine."

Edward nodded. "And you don't trust her."

"Do you?"

He shook his head. "No. I trust your judgment."

Daphne raised her eyebrows, surprised. "Really?"

"Certainly. You're my older sister, and you spent nearly four weeks with our cousins. You had ample time to form an opinion." He flipped closed his book. "Besides, I've been spending time with Wendel, at our club. The stories he tells… He makes them light-hearted, but I can see a trend of selfishness a fathom deep in his sister. Also, and this isn't common knowledge, but Wendel has found out that his father left the estate in rather dire straits. He said he told Cousin Wendy as much, but she makes no attempt to curtail her spending, employing his credit everywhere."

"You spend time with Cousin Wendel?" Daphne leaned forward. "And Mr. Garrick?"

Edward's gaze darted away. "Why do you ask?"

Why should her question inspire such tension? Daphne scrutinized her brother. "Is that a book of sonnets? Shakespeare's?"

Edward flushed. "Maybe."

"You don't read poetry."

"Well, it's damn difficult to around here. All

Father keeps are books on mathematics and the sciences and the natural world. The man never feeds his soul."

An insight hit Daphne. Miss Garrick had admitted to being enamored. "Why are you spending time with Mr. Garrick, Edward?"

He cleared his throat and looked away again. "I didn't say I am."

"You didn't say you are not."

He sighed. "If you must know, I'm smitten with Miss Garrick."

Daphne nodded, pleased she'd guessed.

Edward released a longer sigh. "Have you ever seen such shimmering midnight tresses? Eyes like twin pools of silver? That skin. The grace of her every movement."

Daphne had, indeed, noted beguiling silver eyes and raven hair, but not on Miss Garrick. "You truly have been reading poetry."

"You would too, were you in love. I never understood it before, but now it speaks to me."

Daphne pursed her lips. If her brother and Miss Garrick courted, that would be a connection. A reason to more frequently see Mr. Garrick. "Does she return your affection?"

Edward shook his head, his expression folding into lines of worry. "I've no idea. She always seems pleased to dance with me and seems entertained by my conversation. Not like when she partners Wendel. They hardly speak and they both appear uncomfortable."

Daphne nodded. Should she tell her brother that

Miss Garrick had admitted to an attachment? Her words could spur Edward to action, and what if Miss Garrick had not meant him?

But what if she had? "She admitted to being in love but could not be prevailed upon to give the gentleman's name."

"Truly? When?"

"Some weeks ago."

"But, after we'd met?"

Daphne nodded. "Certainly. I recall thinking at the time that the two of you had already danced on several occasions."

Edward leaned back, expression almost foolish with joy. "She might mean me. She could very well mean me." He stood.

"Where are you going?"

"It's the hour for calling. I will go and discover the truth."

"Right now?" Daphne stared up at him in shock.

Edward nodded. "Right now." He swept a low bow. "By this evening, I will either be the happiest of men or wallowing in misery, and it's all thanks to you, sister dear." He pivoted and strode from the room.

Daphne watched him go, stunned, and filled with dread that his mood that evening would be the latter.

Chapter Seventeen

Arthur closed the final ledger and rubbed his forehead. He'd spent days in his uncle's… rather, his own, office, going over the books his man had provided. This was his third pass. He still couldn't reconcile what he'd learned.

He leaned back in the stiff leather chair, gaze sweeping about the small office. Cramped, really. What had Edward Hayhurst called the townhome? On the edge of what's fashionable? It showed. The furnishings hadn't been replaced, refinished, or reupholstered in Arthur's lifetime. As much as he loved the place that he called home, now that it was his, he could admit that everything was a touch shoddy. A touch small. A bit rundown.

The country manor had been the same. The tenants, conveying hope, had lodged numerous complaints. Their roads were pitted. Several bridges showed rot and had become dangerous to cross. They wished to build a new mill, but his uncle hadn't allocated the funds. Many of the fields were fallow for they routinely only had enough seeds to grow food on which to live, not extra to sell.

And to what end? Uncle Garrick had been wealthy. Despite his uncle's tendency to save, as when he'd fired Lillian's nanny or elected not to send her to the best finishing school, or the nearly embarrassingly small allowance he'd given Arthur on which to live, Arthur had always known as much. Still, he hadn't realized how wealthy.

Now, it all belonged to Arthur. A mixture of elation and shock swirled through him. He was one of the wealthiest men in England. He could buy anything. Do anything.

He sucked in a deep breath. But he shouldn't. He must try to allocate his wealth responsibly. The bridges first, and the roads. Then the mill. A smile cut across his face. Come spring, his tenants would have seeds aplenty. The beautiful old country manor where he and Lillian had resided while they mourned Uncle Garrick would be repaired, the townhome refurbished.

Or should he purchase a new London home? One in a more fashionable location?

Arthur shook his head. No. He didn't wish to reside in London. If he'd learned anything from coming to know the Hayhursts, it was that London and the sort of people who flocked there were to be avoided.

The Hayhursts had found firm purchase in his thoughts while he worked. Rather, one of them in particular. Surely, with his new fortune and his newfound disdain for London society, he could ensure they all weathered any vindictive little spites Wendy might cast at them if he pursued Miss Hayhurst?

Surely, as well, Wendy had found someone else to occupy her by now. She had no way to know quite how wealthy he was. He certainly hadn't.

Nor would he inform anyone.

He narrowed his eyes, gaze fixed on the open office door. Furthermore, he would not renovate the townhome until both he and Lillian married. Arthur had learned his lesson and whatever man captured his sister's affections had best do so out of love. He wouldn't even tell her about the funds. Not yet. He would increase her dowry, but there was no need for her to know that, either.

He pulled out a sheet of paper. Should he increase Lillian's dowry to ten thousand pounds? More? He liked the idea of whoever wed her being shocked when they found out how much his sister was worth.

Footsteps in the hall halted Arthur before he could reach for ink and pen.

A moment later, Charles stood framed in the open door, silver tray in hand, a calling card atop. "Mr. Edward Hayhurst to see you, sir."

"Did he say why?"

"Only that he must speak to you urgently. If I may make mention of it, he seems rather agitated."

A vision of Daphne sprang up in Arthur's mind. "Show him in."

"Very good, sir." Charles disappeared back down the hall.

Arthur drummed his fingers on his chair arm. What could have an agitated Edward Hayhurst at his door? He'd seen the man a mere two nights ago, at their club. Hayhurst had seemed his usual affable self, playing cards, drinking, ribbing Wendel. After an interminable time, two sets of footsteps sounded in the hall.

Charles returned to the doorway to bow. "Mr. Hayhurst, sir," he said as he straightened and stepped aside. "Will you require anything?"

Arthur nodded to Edward Hayhurst as he entered. "Do you need anything other than brandy, Hayhurst?"

"No, thank you, but I would rather care for a snifter, since you mention it. Now that I'm here, I'm struck with nerves."

"I can see to it, Charles." Arthur stood and made his way around the desk to the sideboard.

Charles disappeared back down the hall.

Edward Hayhurst strode deeper into the room, looking about. "Office, I see? Good place for it."

Arthur frowned as he poured. He turned and passed a glass to Hayhurst, asking, "A good place in the house to have an office, or the office is a good place to discuss the reason you've come?"

"Thank you." Hayhurst saluted with his glass, then took a long swig. "Both, I suppose."

Arthur poured a finger full for himself. "And why have you come?"

"Right to it, then?"

Arthur shrugged. "I don't see why not. Care for a seat?"

Hayhurst shook his head. "Best done standing, in case you chase me off. You've half a head on me." He took another drink.

"Chase you off?"

"I'm in love, you see. At least, I think I am."

Arthur raised his glass. "Congratulations, then.

Who is the lucky young woman?"

Hayhurst drained the remainder of his drink. "That's just it, you see. It's your sister. I'm in love with Miss Garrick."

Carefully, Arthur set his glass back on the sideboard. He'd daydreamed about discussing marriage with a Hayhurst, but not this Hayhurst, to be certain. "I beg your pardon?"

"You know, all midnight locks and stormy gray eyes and whatnot."

"I'm aware of Lillian's hair and eye color. She takes after our father."

"As do you. Your uncle as well, as I recall."

Arthur's gaze went to the closed ledgers. "Is this something to do with my uncle's fortune?"

Hayhurst's eyes went wide. "What? Certainly not. I stand to inherit quite a lot, you know."

"I know your father is wealthy. I also know you have six siblings, four of them sisters with large dowries."

"Who told you they have large dowries?" Hayhurst thunked his empty glass down on the sideboard as well.

"You did, you lout. When you chased me from your manor house this past April. Remember?"

Hayhurst took a half step back. "Oh, yes, that's right." He grimaced. "I'm terribly sorry about that." He cleared his throat. "But no, I don't have a clue about Miss Garrick's dowry. It's more about the... the hair and eyes thing."

Arthur stared at the slightly younger man. It wasn't as if Hayhurst was a bad sort. Wendel's cousin. Daphne's younger brother. Lillian could do far worse. "So you're here to…?"

"To, uh, ask your permission to court Miss Garrick."

"I see." A better answer than Arthur had expected. He'd thought Edward Hayhurst more the run-off-with-her-to-Scotland type. "Does my sister return your esteem?"

"I don't really know. She seems cordial enough."

"Cordial?" Arthur supposed cordial could be a fine beginning for a relationship. "How about I send for her and we ask her?" Arthur crossed to the bellpull.

"If she wants to marry me? Isn't that the sort of thing I ought to ask her myself, Garrick?"

"How about we ask her if she's interested in being courted by you first?" Arthur worked to school all amusement from his voice and face. "You can build up to the marrying part."

"Yes. Right. Good idea."

Arthur yanked the bellpull, then returned to the sideboard, where Hayhurst stood, expression nervous. An awkward silence fell, not broken until footsteps sounded in the hall.

A footman stepped into the open doorway. "Sir?"

"Please ask my sister to join us."

"Yes, sir." The footman bowed and disappeared.

Silence returned.

Hayhurst tugged at his cravat.

Arthur gestured to the decanter. "Another?"

Hayhurst shook his head. "Best not."

At least he had sense enough not to get sloshed in the middle of an important conversation. Arthur cast a critical eye over the other man. Nineteen. A bit young to wed, even were it legal to do so without parental permission. About a half head shorter than Arthur, as Hayhurst had earlier noted, but upright and capable seeming enough. "Have you discussed this with your father?"

Hayhurst shook his head. "I didn't think to. I made up my mind and came straight over."

"I see." Arthur didn't truly see. Hayhurst couldn't wed without his father's permission. Was he so certain it would be granted, or too impulsive to care? "Not rushing this, are you? It's not a decision you want to get wrong."

As Arthur almost had. He'd nearly shackled himself to a money grubbing, shrill, ambitious, vindictive woman.

"You don't believe your sister would make me a good wife?" Hayhurst sounded surprised.

"She would make any man a good wife."

Hayhurst nodded.

Silence returned.

Finally, light footfalls heralded Lillian. She entered smiling, her expression turning quizzical when she saw their guest. "You asked to see me, Arthur? Good afternoon, Mr. Hayhurst."

"Mr. Hayhurst has come to me with a quandary for which I require your opinion," Arthur said.

"My opinion?"

He nodded. "He esteems you and wishes to know if he may court you."

Lillian turned wide eyes on Hayhurst. "Oh."

Once more, silence filled the room, oppressive. Lillian stared at the floor. Hayhurst swallowed audibly, his gaze on her.

Arthur endeavored for a light tone, saying, "Your response lacks a certain amount of enthusiasm, Lillian."

She looked up, met Hayhurst's gaze, and grimaced. "I'm sorry. I… you're perfectly pleasant, Mr. Hayhurst. I simply do not feel that way about you. I would still very much like us to be friends."

Arthur winced on Hayhurst's behalf. The exchange perfectly illustrated the sort of conversation he wished to avoid with the fellow's sister. No man wished to be labeled perfectly pleasant.

Hayhurst rubbed the back of his neck. "Ah, yes, well then. Thank you, Miss Garrick, for your time. You as well, Garrick. Sorry to be a bother. I know the way back to the entrance hall. Just… carry on, etcetera." He crossed to the office door.

Lillian hastily stepped aside, for she blocked the way from the room. She cast Arthur a miserable, apologetic look.

Hayhurst went around her but whirled back when he reached the doorway. "Is it something I did? Or said?"

Lillian shook her head. "No. You're always kind and enjoyable to converse with."

He started to turn away again, then came back around. "There's someone else, isn't there? Only, Daphne said you'd admitted to being in love."

Lillian's eyes flew wide. She cast a quick look at Arthur.

Hayhurst followed her gaze. He grimaced. "Right, sorry. I shouldn't have mentioned that. I'll, ah, just…" He slipped from the room.

"I'd best walk him out," Lillian said in a rush.

"Lil." Arthur made sure his tone was firm but not aggravated.

She halted halfway to the door, back to him. "Yes?"

"Are you in love?"

"That Miss Hayhurst is a terrible gossip. First, she told Wendy about Christine's Mr. Quincy, and now she told her brother that I fancy someone. She's no right to spread such tales."

"That doesn't answer my question."

Lillian smoothed her skirt. "Yes. If you must know, there is someone I esteem."

"Will you tell me who?"

She glanced over her shoulder, expression stubborn. "Not yet."

Arthur studied her for a long moment. He recognized the set of her jaw from their uncle and, were he being honest, from the mirror. Stubbornness must be passed down along with the gray eyes and black hair that marked the Garrick line. "Will you give me your word to do nothing rash?"

She turned to face him fully. "Yes. Of course. I

wouldn't do anything troublesome, Arthur."

"Very well, then."

Lillian awarded him a watery smile and slipped from the room.

Arthur didn't care for not knowing on whom his sister had settled her heart. He'd best interview Mrs. Smith. Perhaps she would have insight. He would also need to attend more events with Lillian, rather than leaving her in the care of her chaperone. Until Lillian wished to share the gentleman's name, Arthur had best guard her closely.

And if attending more events put him more in the way of a certain caramel coiffed miss, he supposed he would have to be content with that.

Chapter Eighteen

Daphne looked about the crowded ballroom, somewhat less awed than when they'd first arrived in London. Halfway through December, much of the shine of the Season had worn off. Each event featured most of the same participants. At every dance, the same gentlemen partnered her. While several showed determination in their interest, none of them made her heart skip about in her chest, or caused the room to possess a swirling, giddy feel. At least, none save one, and he rarely attended. Even so, her gaze skimmed over the crowd, seeking a tall gentleman with raven-black hair.

"Ugh," Edward said beside her. "Garrick is here. That can only mean his sister is as well. Perhaps I'll go to my club."

Heartbeat speeding up, Daphne peered in the direction her brother looked but, not being as tall as Edward, she couldn't see them. "Don't be that way, Edward. You can't hope to avoid them forever."

"It's your fault I wish to avoid them at all. You said she esteemed me."

Daphne bit her lip. She should not have said anything. She'd gossiped, and for purely selfish reasons. Now Edward paid the price. "I didn't say that. I said she admitted affection for someone."

"Either way, I can't be around her now. I professed affection and she said she didn't return it.

Or, rather, Garrick professed it for me. It's all terribly embarrassing."

"Did you ever consider that, maybe, if you'd professed it yourself, you may have received a different answer?"

Edward grimaced. "Yes, well, I thought I was in love when I went over there, but the closer it came to the time to say it, the harder it got to get the words out."

"Do you truly blame her, then?"

He shrugged. "It's not a question of blame, except for your part in it. It's a question of pride."

Daphne rolled her eyes. "Yes. Delicate male pride."

"Daphne, Edward, have you seen your sister?" their mother's voice, pitched low, said from behind them.

Daphne turned with a frown. "She was with you."

"You two went to get punch," Edward added.

Mother shrugged. "Yes, but I saw your aunt and we fell into conversation, and I seem to have misplaced your sister."

"She can't have got far." Edward glanced about. "We'll help you look."

"Thank you," Mother said. "I'll go back to the refreshments."

"We'll search the ballroom," Daphne said.

Edward offered his arm and they began a slow circuit of the room.

Daphne noticed he led them away from where he'd spotted Mr. Garrick. "She may be with Mr.

Garrick, you know. She's quite close with Miss Garrick."

"I can see that she's not. Miss Garrick and her chaperone are walking away from him, though. I suppose speaking with Garrick wouldn't be too bad if she's still absent when we reach that side of the room."

Much as she wished to see Mr. Garrick, Daphne accepted Edward's stipulation, aware she was somewhat at fault for his predicament. They circumnavigated the room at a slow pace. She didn't see Christine anywhere.

Edward drew to a halt outside the series of rooms set aside for women to refresh themselves and nodded to the doorway. "Check in there. I'll wait."

"I won't be long."

The first room, designed for the purpose with pink-silk clad walls, an abundance of mirrors, and chairs with decorative embroidered pillows, held nearly as dense a crowd as the ballroom. Daphne pressed through, scanning the clumps of women, both seated and standing.

She pressed between two matronly women and spotted Christine near the back of the room, with Wendy and Miss Garrick. As Daphne watched, her sister handed a folded note to Cousin Wendy. Wendy offered a sweet smile that Daphne trusted not at all. She pressed forward but failed to reach them before Wendy tucked the note away.

"Cousin Wendy, Miss Garrick," Daphne greeted with forced affability. "I do not wish to interrupt, but our mother is looking for Christine."

"Looking for me? I've only been from her side for a moment. Besides, Mrs. Smith is here." She gestured to Miss Garrick's portly chaperone, who sat in a chair against the wall, chatting with another woman.

Trying to ignore Miss Garrick's frown, for ever since Edward's rebuffed declaration, Miss Garrick had looked at her that way, Daphne said, "Yes, but you aren't meant to go off unchaperoned."

"You're unchaperoned," Cousin Wendy pointed out.

"Edward waits without." Daphne immediately wished to call the words back, as Miss Garrick's frown deepened. She sucked in a breath. "Look, Miss Garrick, I'm very sorry I told Edward that you esteem someone. I should not have said that."

Cool gray eyes studied her. "No. You should not have."

An agony of embarrassment and remorse twisting inside her, Daphne said, "If I could take it back, I truly would."

"But you cannot," Wendy said primly. "Which is why you should not gossip."

Heat filled Daphne's cheeks. It mortified her that Wendy was right.

Miss Garrick let out a sigh. "Did you truly believe I fancied Edward?"

Daphne nodded. "At least, I hoped you did. You always seem to enjoy dancing with him, and you and Christine have become such dear friends. I thought it would be pleasant to have you for a sister."

"It would be," Christine added.

Much of the frost melted from Miss Garrick's expression. "It would have been pleasant, I agree. You have such a large family. Arthur and I have always been alone, except for our uncle."

"And the gentleman you esteem doesn't have a large family?" Cousin Wendy asked, a sharp edge to her tone.

Miss Garrick turned a beatific smile on her. "I did not say that."

It pleased Daphne to realize that Wendy hadn't yet ferreted out Miss Garrick's secret. Not knowing must be driving Wendy mad. But as much as she enjoyed watching Wendy stew, she touched Christine's arm. "Mother is worried."

Christine heaved a sigh. "I'd best go reassure her. Will you both call tomorrow for tea?"

Wendy shrugged. "Perhaps. If I find time. I have so very many calls to return."

Beside her, where Wendy couldn't see, Miss Garrick rolled her eyes.

"Yes, well, hopefully we will see you," Daphne said and looped her arm through her sister's. "If you'll both excuse us." She led her sister away through the crowded room, but as soon as they were out of earshot, she leaned close and whispered, "I saw you hand Wendy a note."

Christine cast her an annoyed look. "So?"

"So, it cannot have been a note for Miss Garrick. She stood with you both." Daphne held her breath.

"It was nothing."

"It must have been something."

Christine pulled her arm away. "Nothing to

concern you. You aren't my mother. Lately, you're hardly even my friend, which I suppose you'll prove by telling Mother all about it." She pushed through the doorway and strode out into the ballroom.

Daphne realized she'd halted and resumed her steps to hurry after Christine. She resisted the urge to blot her eyes, blinking rapidly instead. She and Christine had never been close, the way Justina and Katherine were, but they'd always been friends.

"There you are," Edward said. He nodded deeper into the ballroom, to where their mother spoke with Mr. Garrick, Christine's retreating form moving in their direction. "Christine went on to Mother. You will join them?"

"You won't?"

He looked past her. "Will Miss Garrick come through that doorway soon, now that Christine has?"

Daphne considered. "She may. She seemed a bit tired of Wendy's pomposity."

Edward nodded. "Well then, no, I will not join you in conversation with Garrick."

"I apologized to Miss Garrick. She seems accepting of what transpired."

Edward raised an eyebrow. "Did you? You never apologized to me."

Daphne let out a sigh. "I am very sorry for the entire incident. I should never have become involved, or involved you."

Edward nodded. "Good enough. I'd actually planned to go over to Garrick's townhome already. I simply hadn't selected the proper day."

Daphne resisted the urge to punch him in the

shoulder. They were, after all, in a crowded ballroom. "Then it's hardly my fault."

He shrugged. "It could be. I may have changed my mind without you spurring me. Come to my senses and all that. Go. I'll chaperone you from here until you reach Christine and Mother, then I'll be on my way."

As she did, indeed, wish to speak with Mr. Garrick, Daphne decided to let Edward have his way. She set off after Christine, who, even then, curtsied to Mr. Garrick. He bowed to her but, when he straightened, he caught Daphne's eye. A smile pulled at her lips as a light, bubbly feeling coursed through her.

She reached them and mimicked her sister's curtsy.

"Miss Hayhurst, Miss Christine, I would be honored if you would each consent to a set." As he spoke, his gaze held Daphne's.

"I've promised mine away, I'm afraid," Christine said, taking a half step back. "You must be content with Daphne." A quick look showed that her sister and mother exchanged an inscrutable look. "Maybe, as I am unavailable, you will even have to dance two sets with her."

Mr. Garrick didn't even look at Christine, his attention focused on Daphne. "Maybe. Let us begin with one set, shall we, Miss Hayhurst?" He proffered his arm.

Daphne took it, feeling as if her entire being trembled imperceptibly. Mr. Garrick hadn't disagreed with the idea. Nor had he said yes.

"If you will excuse us, Mrs. Hayhurst, Miss Christine?" Mr. Garrick said.

Daphne's relations murmured their assent as he led her away. She cast him a nervous glance, suddenly unsure how to behave. Had he meant… was he interested? So, he truly had given up all love for Wendy? Daphne did a rapid count. It was over six months since Wendy had refused his offer. Still, if he'd truly loved her, should his love be so fickle?

"You are counting under your breath, Miss Hayhurst," Mr. Garrick said as they took their place with the other dancers.

To her pleasure, the musicians struck up a minuet. Her cheeks heated, though whether from his question or memories of their first dance, alone under the blue spring sky, she couldn't sort out. "I counted the months since we first met."

"That is of interest to you?"

She nodded.

"It was the beginning of April," he offered. "Well over six months ago."

"You seem a different man now than then."

He frowned slightly as they executed a stately turn. "I have endured several… difficult experiences since that day." He met her gaze when they switched hands. "I suppose I have learned a great deal about who I am. That ought to make a man change, do you not think?"

She nodded. "I do."

"But you do not approve of the change?"

"I…" Did a way exist to discover how deeply he'd cared for her cousin without insulting him?

Given her recent inability to speak of aught but the weather without upsetting those for whom she cared, Daphne was unsure.

"That was a very brief answer, Miss Hayhurst."

Daphne's face heated. "I do not wish to upset you, sir."

"Then do not say what it is you would say." He shook his head, expression grim. "I have endured enough disappointment for the time being."

Daphne swallowed. "I certainly would not wish to add to that, Mr. Garrick."

"I thank you."

They proceeded through the dance, and the next, in near silence. Pain writhed in Daphne's gut. By the time he returned her to her mother and sister, she felt she might cry. She hadn't gossiped this time. She hadn't attempted to spur anyone into doing anything. Yet, she'd still managed to ruin everything. Mr. Garrick politely bid her mother, her sister, and her good evening, then turned and walked away. Daphne could only watch, wondering if she would ever see him again.

Chapter Nineteen

Arthur wandered into the breakfast parlor late in the morning and crossed the room to slump into his chair. "Coffee, please," he said, not looking at the footman who hovered nearby, and reached for his paper.

"You've been coming to breakfast later and later each day," Lillian said.

He blinked. He hadn't even noticed his sister seated at the other end of the table. "Have I?"

"You've also stopped going out."

"Hm." He shook open the paper. Coffee appeared at his elbow.

"What happened?"

Arthur sighed and put down the paper. "Nothing."

Lillian narrowed her eyes. "Something happened."

Arthur permitted a bitter chuckle. "No. Nothing happened. That's the trouble."

"You are being deliberately confusing."

He scrubbed a hand across his forehead. "I thought something would happen. Instead, nothing happened."

"Does this have to do with a certain miss?"

Arthur darted a look about the room, suddenly acutely aware of not only the footman but also of two maids. "If it does, she will remain nameless."

Lillian nodded. "May I ask, then, if this nameless miss refused you?"

He shook his head. "I made no offer for her to refuse."

Lillian frowned. She picked up a piece of toast and took a bite, expression contemplative.

Arthur reached for the paper.

"If you made no offer, how could anything happen?"

He left the paper on the table and picked up his coffee instead. "I believe my comments made it quite clear that I held an interest in pursuing more."

Wide eyes blinked at him. "You believe?"

He shrugged. "I hinted that I might partner the miss in question twice in one evening. That should be clear enough."

"That would be, if you had partnered her twice. Perhaps your hint was too vague." Those eyes narrowed again. "You aren't usually vague."

Arthur grimaced. "Yes, well, I didn't feel the need to expose myself to torment so I put forth the suggestion of two sets. She replied that she did not wish to upset me. I took that as a kindness on her part."

"Oh." Lillian took another bite of toast. "Is this how you were after Wendy threw you over, then? All moping and miserable to be around?"

"No, I—" How had he been? He shook his head. "No. I was shocked. I went out for a ride." He'd felt betrayed. Humiliated. Confused. "Maybe I didn't really believe her?"

"So, later, once you felt that she meant it, then

you were sad?"

Arthur took a sip of coffee. No. He hadn't been sad. Not as he was now. He hadn't had this deep, abiding feeling of loss. This suspicion that his life would be empty forever. Incomplete. Never whole, because he'd missed something. Lost something irreplaceable. He swallowed and reached for his paper.

"Arthur?"

"Let me read the paper, Lillian," he muttered and flipped it open.

"What's that?" his sister asked.

Arthur clamped his mouth closed over a reply. Couldn't she leave him to his sorrow?

"Arthur?" Urgency, near panic, filled his sister's voice.

He slapped the paper down. "Yes?"

"Turn over the paper."

Was that fear in his sister's voice? Arthur turned the paper over to skim the back.

He breathed a curse, causing his sister's eyes to further widen.

Taking up half a page, the paper featured a reproduction of a letter. The names were abbreviated, but it was very clear the letter was from Miss Christine Hayhurst to her lover, Mr. Ryan Quincy, a former lieutenant. The letter, in no uncertain terms, begged Mr. Quincy to run off to Scotland with her, as soon as possible and in direct defiance of her father.

"Is that by whom I think it's by?" Lillian whispered.

Arthur looked up to see his sister's face as pale as the table linen. "She's ruined," he breathed.

Lillian gripped the edge of the table with white fingers. "Does it say where the paper got the letter? Or… or why they would print such a thing?"

Arthur skimmed the page. "It says a concerned citizen, who does not wish to see upright young women corrupted, submitted the letter so that civilized society would know of a viper in its midst." He looked up to find Lillian biting her lower lip. "It was Wendy, wasn't it?"

His sister shook her head. "It… it could be. She… she's been passing letters between Christine and her beau." Her voice dropped to a whisper. "She said she wanted to help. That because she'd been denied her true love, didn't mean Christine should be."

Arthur bit back another curse. "She also said she would get even with me for refusing to marry her."

Lillian's eyes flew wide. "She said that?"

He nodded. "The day you tried to arrange for us to reconcile."

His sister went red. "Oh."

"Was Barlow in on it?"

"M-Mr. Barlow? On the letters?"

Arthur shook his head, thoughtful. "No. I know he wouldn't do this." He tapped the paper. "Did he agree to help you get Wendy and me to reconcile? He made no bones about going to the library with you. In the past, he wouldn't have left his sister unchaperoned with me."

"I—yes."

Had the Hayhursts seen the paper yet? Of course they had. How must they feel? And Daphne. This was her Season, too. She would never make a match now. Elation shot through him, followed hard by shame. Much as he couldn't bear the thought of her with another man, he'd rather that she find someone than end up alone. They shouldn't both have to suffer that fate.

He surged to his feet. "I should go to them. Offer what assistance I can. I cannot help but feel somewhat responsible."

Lillian stood as well, wringing her hands. "Do you think that Wendy did this? If so, then I am to blame as well. I assured Christine that she could trust Wendy."

Arthur strode the length of the table. "Stay here. I'll see what may be accomplished."

"If you see Christine, please tell her I am sorry," Lillian beseeched as he passed.

He nodded and gestured for the waiting footman to follow him from the room. Sending the man for his horse, Arthur hurried to his chamber to change. Somehow, Stenson already waited with appropriate garb. In short order, Arthur rode to London's most prosperous street.

As the fashionable areas of London were generally quiet in the morning hours, it took little time to reach the Hayhurst household, but Arthur had to knock twice before the door cracked open and a harried looking butler peeked out.

"Can I help you, sir?"

"I'm here to see Miss Hayhurst," Arthur replied,

unsure for whom to ask. "Tell her it's Mr. Garrick."

"Garrick, is that you?" The butler stepped back as the door jerked wider to reveal Edward Hayhurst. "It is. Come in. You've heard? Hell of a mess, this." Hayhurst backed into the entrance hall as he spoke.

Arthur stepped inside and began stripping off his outerwear, which he handed to the disgruntled butler. Despite the butler's appearance, the house proved oddly silent. Eerily so.

"Good of you to come over," Hayhurst said, gesturing for Arthur to follow him. "What with us being on the out and out." He shot Arthur a grimace. "Especially after my visit a few weeks ago."

Arthur raised an eyebrow. "And the way you've avoided me since?"

"Yes, and that."

They entered a well appointed parlor, recently redone to the height of fashion. Edward Hayhurst didn't sit, instead pacing across the room. "Don't know what Christine was thinking. And that cousin of ours, she's a piece of work, but I don't have to tell you that."

Arthur remained immediately inside the doorway, to give Hayhurst room to pace. "I worry I am partly at fault."

Edward Hayhurst stopped mid stride and whirled back. "You're at fault? How's that?"

"Miss Barlow threatened to make me pay if I did not wed her. She specifically mentioned driving your family from London as, in her words, her father had done."

Hayhurst shook his head and resumed his pacing. "Not your fault, then. You can't be expected to marry such a vile woman. Certainly not for our sakes." He shook his head. "Vindictive shrew, our cousin."

"Regardless of blame, I came to see if there is aught I can do."

"Not likely, is it? Meaning no offense, but what can anyone do?"

"Someone could go and get Quincy, and make him do right by your sister."

Edward Hayhurst shook his head yet again. "I'd rather go challenge him," he muttered, then sighed. "He's an old friend, but writing to Christine in secret? That's too much."

"No one is to go to challenge Mr. Quincy." Daphne's voice brought Arthur around to face the hallway. "Good morning, Mr. Garrick. It's good of you to come." Her amber eyes were red-rimmed, her cheeks devoid of color.

Arthur longed to pull her into his arms, to offer comfort. Instead, he bowed. "Good morning, Miss Hayhurst."

She looked past him, to her brother. "The letter was from Christine to Mr. Quincy. We don't even know if he's involved."

"You know what Father believes."

"And you know what Mother and I believe. What you seem to have forgotten is that Father waits for you in the entrance hall."

"Right." Edward Hayhurst hurried across the

room. "I forgot I awaited him there. Off to talk to our man about charges of defamation, for what good it will do." He nodded to Arthur and left the room.

Arthur turned to Daphne. Would she ask him to go?

"Walk with me in the garden, Mr. Garrick?"

He nodded.

She led the way to the back of the townhome and through a door. They entered a well cared for garden which was undoubtedly lovely when verdant. Now, it proved stark and rather cold. He offered Daphne his arm, noting that she wore no cloak or even a shawl. She stood close as they set out down a gravel path, likely for warmth.

He worked to organize his thoughts, difficult when she stood so near that he could smell the lemon-honey scent of her hair. "I'm sorry," he began.

Daphne shook her head. In the wan sunlight, her curls gleamed with hints of gold. "I can't see how this is your fault," she said, much as her brother had. "Given the longstanding rift between our families, we should have been warier of our cousins."

"How is Miss Christine? Lillian asked after her as well."

"That's kind of your sister. I wish I could say Christine is bearing up but, in truth, she's been crying all morning."

"Surely, your father will now see that Mr. Quincy weds her. Is that not what both wish for?"

Daphne angled her head to gaze up through leafless branches. The crushed stone that lined the walk crunched beneath their feet. "Father believes this a plot on Christine's part, or perhaps hers and Mr. Quincy's together, to force him to permit them to wed before Mr. Quincy has paid his debts. He remains adamant that they will not marry until Mr. Quincy and his estate are no longer at risk. He says he would rather see his daughter disgraced than wed to a man in debtors' prison."

"Debts? I thought your father simply wished Miss Christine to meet more gentlemen before making her choice."

Daphne shook her head. "He does, but the stipulation he put on their wedding concerns debt. Mr. Quincy's older brother mortgaged the lands and borrowed heavily. Father decreed that Christine couldn't wed Mr. Quincy so long as her dowry would go to paying his debts instead of ensuring a secure future for her and any children she may bear. According to rumor, her dowry is nearly the exact amount he owes." She cast Arthur a quick look, blushing. "It isn't truly gossiping to tell you. I mean, it's common knowledge around our country seat."

"I can see why your father might suspect a conspiracy, then. You and your mother disagree?"

"We were all at breakfast when Father read the letter. Christine is not so good an actress as to fake her horror."

"Perhaps your father may be persuaded?"

"I do not know. I believe he would take her side

were he not so angry. I've never seen him so enraged."

Sharp and hard, fear jolted through Arthur on Daphne's behalf. "He's not… volatile?"

She shook her head. "No. He's angry with himself, I think. For letting our family associate with the Barlows again. He's declared that none of us may even be in the same room with them, but I find it difficult to believe Wendel or my aunt had aught to do with publicizing Christine's letter. Not that it matters."

"Surely it matters. If they are innocent, they should not know censure."

"I mean, rather, that it does not matter what restrictions Father places. There's been a parade of messengers all morning, rescinding and declining invitations. We will have nowhere to go, and so will not need to worry over seeing my aunt or cousins."

He halted them before a low stone bench and turned to face her. "Will you leave London?"

Sorrow filled her eyes. "I'm not certain. I imagine so."

Arthur stared down into those amber eyes and fought for control. If only she would give him some inkling, some indication of shared attraction between them, he would kiss the sorrow from her. Slowly, almost against his will, he leaned closer.

He should look away. He knew that. Yet, as he'd found before, Daphne Hayhurst affected him like no other woman ever had. Her presence drove away the reason with which he usually governed his life.

Now, on top of her usual allure, she appeared hurt. In need of comfort.

"And how are you bearing up?" he asked, speaking in an attempt to give his lips any other task than kissing her, but he knew the words weren't enough.

He must think of some topic that would quench his ardor. Especially with her sister's scandal, propriety must be obeyed.

Chapter Twenty

Daphne stared up at Mr. Garrick, unable to move. He'd asked a question, but her mind provided no reply. All she could think about was what his lips might feel like pressed to hers. He leaned nearer still, dark locks falling forward across his forehead. Any moment now, he was going to kiss her. Her heart pounded so fiercely, he must surely hear its frantic beat. A shiver of delight coursed through her frame.

He went still. "You're cold."

She shook her head, the gesture nearly imperceptible as his lips, so near, seemed to pull hers to them, prohibiting other movement.

"You shivered."

Heat suffused her cheeks. She had shivered but she would surely die of embarrassment if she told him why. "I'm not cold."

"Let me judge." Warm hands slid up her arms and came to rest on her shoulders. Lifting a hand, he stroked the backs of his fingers across her cheek. "I've never felt anything so soft," he murmured, gaze roaming over her. His other hand reached to cup the back of her neck, under her curls. "No, not cold."

"I told you."

"So you did."

Her heart fluttered like a caged bird. If he didn't

kiss her soon, she felt certain she would faint, but all he did was stand there, lips a whisper away, his breath a warm caress scented with fresh coffee and cinnamon.

"What was it you wished to say?" he said.

"Say?" Did he truly want an answer to his earlier question? What had he even asked? How she fared in light of the scandal?

"When last we danced, some few weeks ago, you began to say something to me."

Daphne blinked several times. "That is important now?"

"It seemed very important to you at the time. I believe not voicing it ruined our set."

She looked down, then realized that her palms rested against his waistcoat. Somehow, she'd slid her hands inside his jacket. She jerked them back, aghast.

"I'm sorry. I didn't realize I was—" Her cheeks heated to a level of warmth surely congruent with that of the sun. "I didn't mean to place my hands on you."

"As I placed my hands on you, it seems only fair."

She took a step back, the hand cupping her neck falling to his side. "What am I doing? My family is already embroiled in scandal."

His expression darkened. "So you think this," he gestured between them, "is only destined for scandal?"

"That is not what I meant." How did she always manage to say the wrong thing?

He tugged at his coat, then pressed a hand through his hair, pushing it back into place. "I… I should go. We ought not to be here alone, unchaperoned."

"You can see the whole garden from the house." Her eyes flew wide at her own words. She peered past him. All the windows appeared empty.

"You look very relieved," he said in a tight voice.

Daphne kept her lips pressed closed. Anything she said would be the wrong thing.

Mr. Garrick let out an explosive breath. "You confuse me, Miss Hayhurst."

"I confuse you?" Had she heard aright? "You confuse me, sir."

"In what way?"

"For a start, in the way I nearly mentioned when we danced." Although, confusion didn't seem quite the right word to describe her worry. Still, he'd asked, and now she was irked. "Six months past, you loved my cousin. How can I know anything you feel for me will not be as fleeting?"

His expression hardened with anger. "That is your worry? That I would kiss you and not wed you?"

Daphne shook her head. "I worry more that you would kiss me, wed me, and tire of me in half a year."

A frown marred his lips. "So, you fear I am fickle."

She issued a shaky nod.

Eyes flinty, he said, "Yet, I believe you would

have kissed me."

Daphne squared her shoulders. "Because I, sir, am not fickle." She stepped around him, meaning to charge into the house.

A hand caught her arm but didn't turn her. He leaned close to speak low and fast in her ear. "Nor am I. For all I thought myself infatuated with Miss Barlow for years, she could never move me as you do. Alone in the garden, she begged for a kiss. I believe I knew even then, deep down, that I did not love her. That is why it was so easy not to kiss her."

Without turning back, Daphne said, "Alone in the garden with me, you seem to find equal restraint. I believe you know your way to the front door." She yanked free of his grip and hurried to the house.

No footfalls followed. No words called her back. She longed to read the expression on his face but feared to turn around. One look into those stormy gray eyes could be her undoing.

Inside, she slipped immediately up the back stairwell, the servants' stairs, afraid Mr. Garrick would follow. In the near darkness, she climbed to the second floor, dashing tears from her cheeks. She spilled out into the upper hall and drew in a deep, steadying breath, then went down the hall in the direction of her room.

As she passed her sister's door, Daphne heard the unmistakable sound of crying. She clenched her teeth and kept walking. Christine had created her own torment and she'd made her feelings for Daphne clear enough of late.

Daphne halted.

She would have kissed Mr. Garrick in the garden. In that moment, with a certainty, she would have abandoned propriety for love. Which apparently, by his measure, meant what she felt for him was real. Christine's affection for Mr. Quincy had lasted for years. So far as Daphne knew, writing him letters was her only impropriety.

She returned to her sister's room and knocked softly. "Christine?"

The sobs inside muffled but no reply came. Daphne tried the handle to find the door unlocked. She pressed it open and peeked in.

Her sister sat atop a rumpled coverlet, legs pulled up to her chest and arms wrapped about them. Her head, which rested on her crossed arms, came up as the door opened, revealing a blotchy, tear-streaked face framed by limp yellow curls. "Go away. I don't need a lecture, Daphne."

Daphne slipped into the room and closed the door behind her. "I didn't come to lecture."

"Of course you did." Christine let out a sigh and wiped at bloodshot eyes. "Say whatever it is and leave."

"I'm sorry."

"Sorry?"

Daphne nodded. She moved closer slowly, like she cornered a spooked cat, and said, "Sorry that I didn't work harder to make Cousin Wendy like me, so she wouldn't be so mean. Sorry I didn't try harder to keep you away from her, or to be a better sister so you could have come to me." She sat down on the bed next to her sister, hands limp in her lap. "Most of all, I'm sorry Father won't simply let you marry Mr. Quincy. You love him. You should get to be happy."

Christine let out a sigh. "I do love him. I don't know why Father won't believe me."

"Because you are young and when he was young, he didn't know what he wanted."

"I didn't plot to have that letter published," Christine whispered.

Daphne put an arm about her. "I know."

Christine tipped her head to rest against Daphne's shoulder. "If Father really won't let Ryan marry me, what's to happen to me?"

Daphne shook her head. "Father cannot remain angry forever. Obviously you and Mr. Quincy should wed."

Christine nodded. She wiped at her eyes again. "You and Mother will champion me?"

"Certainly."

"I didn't mean to ruin your Season."

Daphne laughed, the sound brittle. "I believe I've been doing a fine job of that myself. You didn't ruin it for me."

Christine lifted her head and turned to face Daphne. "But I thought you and Mr. Garrick… that you're fond of each other."

"I'm fond of him. I've no idea if he's fond of me."

"Lillian believes he is."

Daphne shrugged. She blinked several times, feeling her own rush of tears. "That reminds me,

Miss Garrick sends her regards."

Christine appeared to brighten at that. "Does she? Do you think she will still remain friends?"

After how she'd parted with Mr. Garrick moments ago, Daphne wasn't certain he would let his sister associate with them, but she said, "Why wouldn't she? Were we not her friends when no one would speak with her?"

"But that didn't last long, and this is much worse than the rumors Cousin Wendy spread about Mr. Garrick. It was also before Edward tried to court Miss Garrick. I wouldn't blame her if she never again wishes to speak with me."

Daphne squeezed her sister's shoulders. "Well, I would. Now, let's send for water and a hot iron. We should bathe your face and fix your hair. Then we will go to find Mother. Father will return eventually. When he does, we'll make him see reason."

Christine turned and wrapped her in a hug. "Thank you, Daphne."

Chapter Twenty-One

Arthur arrived at his townhome in a foul mood. He barely acknowledged the groom he handed his mount off to, then turned to the front steps.

"Mr. Garrick," a familiar feminine voice called, halting him before he could ascend to the front door.

Arthur turned slowly, a scowl pulling at his mouth. The Barlows' carriage rumbled down the street, Wendy's head protruding from the window. Arthur cast a look up the steps. Should he enter and lock the door behind him?

"Mr. Garrick," she called again, waving, voice and expression light.

Arthur studied her as the carriage halted. She opened the door and waited. Arthur didn't move forward to hand her down. Finally, a frown flickered across her face. She gestured to a footman, who came over to hand her out. Behind her in the dark of the carriage, someone shifted. Wendy came forward to curtsy. Arthur didn't bow.

"Mr. Garrick, how pleasant to see you." Wendy's voice held forced cheer. "Although I must say, I'm a bit put out that you didn't help me down."

"What do you want, Miss Barlow?"

She darted a glance up and down the street. Though the areas stood barely on the edge of what was fashionable, as the day wore on, more and more people were about.

"I would rather speak inside, in private."

"You will never again set foot in my home."

"Do not take that tone with me, Mr. Garrick, for once we are wed, I will not permit you to forget this."

A bark of laughter burst from him. "Wed? You and me? Don't be ridiculous."

Her blue eyes glinted like rare gems. "Listen to me, Arthur. You and I, we are made for one another."

"Ludicrous."

Anger flashed across her features. She drew in a deep breath, then another, then leaned closer to look up at him through her lashes. "Remember how things were? How easy we were with one another? How pleasant? We can have that back."

"I don't want that back. Not with you."

Wendy's eyes narrowed. "Well, you'll never have it with her," she hissed. "Do you think anyone will receive your sister if you ally yourself with the Hayhursts now? Lillian will die unloved and alone."

Arthur didn't honor that with a reply. Instead, he watched Wendy struggle to bring her emotions back under control.

"I realize that somehow, despite how unappealing she is, my cousin has cast a spell over you," Wendy continued in a low voice. "But you will be free of her now. The Hayhursts won't dare show their faces in polite society. Her hold over you will fade. When it does, you'll come back where you belong." She glared at him for a moment longer, tossed her curls, and turned away.

"I have no notion if I will ever see Miss Hayhurst again," Arthur said.

Halfway back to the carriage, Wendy froze.

Arthur didn't raise his voice but made no effort to conceal his words from those few others on the street. "Whether I do or not changes nothing between us, Miss Barlow. You cast me aside the moment you thought I wouldn't secure my uncle's fortune, then came running back as soon as I did, and I'm not even angry with you for that. You did me a favor by revealing your true nature before I made the mistake of wedding you. What I am, and likely always will be angry about, is how you have treated Miss Christine. She didn't deserve your venom or duplicity."

Wendy whirled and marched back up to him. "Neither does Lillian, but I will unleash it on her if you do not come back to me, Arthur. Bear that in mind as you consider your courtship of me."

She strode, straight backed, to the carriage. Not waiting for assistance, she clambered in and slammed the door closed. A sharp order sounded and the conveyance lurched forward.

Voices raised inside, Wendy's and her brother's. The carriage door flew open again. Vehicle still in motion, Wendel jumped out. He landed with a clatter, sighted Arthur, and jogged back down the street.

Arthur grimaced. He'd no desire to speak to any

Barlow. He turned and tramped up the steps to his townhome. The door swung open. Arthur stepped inside. Charles made to swing the door closed, but it bounced back with a grunt. Arthur looked down to see a foot in the doorway.

The door pressed open and Wendel stepped inside. "That rather hurt, you know."

Arthur yanked off his hat and handed it to Charles. "What do you want, Wendel?"

"Look, you must know I didn't know about Wendy's plan."

"Must I?" Arthur asked as he stripped off his gloves.

Wendel's expression firmed from entreaty to indignation. "Yes, you must."

Arthur finally met Wendel's gaze. "Supposing I do, what difference does it make?"

"You can't hold it against a man, the things his sister does."

"Can't I?"

"No. You can't."

Arthur rubbed his forehead. "Look, I don't hold it against you. I simply do not feel charitable enough to entertain any Barlow right now."

"Right now? But not always?"

"For heaven's sake, man, I broke things off with her, not with you. If you're willing to overlook my splitting with your sister, I am."

Wendel let out a relieved breath. "Good, because I heard what she said about Miss Garrick. I don't mean to let any harm come to your sister."

"That's good of you, but I don't see what you

can do outside of locking Miss Barlow away. She's one and twenty now and has resources of her own."

"I can… I can think of a way to protect Miss Garrick's reputation, and repair Miss Christine's."

Arthur winged an eyebrow upward. "Oh?"

"They must both marry."

His second eyebrow joined the first. "And who will they marry?"

"Miss Christine should marry that Quincy fellow. I read her letter. She's clearly in love with him. He's a cad if he doesn't come through for her. I'm only her cousin but, if Edward doesn't, I'll go challenge the bounder."

"Miss Christine's father continues to forbid the union."

"Is my uncle daft?"

"More likely, he's trying to protect his daughter. Quincy's debts are rumored to run about the same amount as Miss Christine's dowry. A jaded man might question whether or not he loves her."

Wendel frowned. "I do recall Mother and Wendy saying something about my uncle forbidding the union, but under the present circumstances, isn't he willing to bend?"

"Apparently not. He's your uncle. Go and speak with him."

Wendel grimaced. "He'll want to see me even less than you do." He cleared his throat. "What about Lil—that is, Miss Garrick, then? Uncle Hayhurst isn't her guardian. You are. You could see her married and away from this trouble."

"Married to whom? She hasn't even admitted a

name to me. How can I know if the gentleman she esteems is worthy?"

"Well, ah, you get on with him well enough."

Arthur took in Wendel's convulsive swallow. His sallow complexion. The way he clenched and unclenched his hands. "You devil. If you lay a finger on m—"

"I didn't." Wendel brought his hands up, palms out, to fend Arthur off. "I wouldn't. I mean, rather, I would, but I… well, I did kiss her."

Arthur's fist collided with Wendel's jaw.

He flew backward, head slamming into the door, then slumped against it. He blinked rapidly.

Arthur strode forward, fist raised.

"Arthur," Lillian cried. Suddenly she was there, arms wrapped about his, weighing down his upraised fist. "Stop."

"He kissed you?"

Lillian stared up at him, tears flooding from her eyes. "No. I kissed him."

Arthur jerked back. "How could you?"

She squared her shoulders, standing tall between him and Wendel, who shook his head as if trying to rattle his brain into place. "I love him. We mean to marry."

Anger and betrayal swirled through Arthur. All those years he'd promised to court Wendy, he'd never touched her. Not once, and Wendel was kissing his little sister? And she'd encouraged him? He pointed up the steps. "To your room."

"Arthur, we're in love. We truly are. Wendel wished to tell you, but I said we must wait until things were settled between you and Wendy."

"Go to your room. Now." Fury filled his voice, low and controlled.

"I will, but only because you are unreasonable at this time," Lillian said. "We will talk more about this later." She strode forward and jabbed a finger into Arthur's chest, her expression suffused with nearly as much anger as he felt. "And do not dare to hurt Wendel again. If you do, I will never, ever forgive you." Lillian marched past Arthur and up the stairs.

Beside the newel post, Charles endeavored to look small.

Arthur turned back to Wendel. "Get out."

Wendel pushed himself upright, rubbing his jaw. "I do love her, you know."

"If you loved her, you would respect her. You would have come to me and asked to court her."

Wendel grimaced. "I won't give up."

"Yes. Tenacity seems to be a Barlow family trait. Get out."

"I'll come back. We can talk about this tomorrow."

"We're leaving London tomorrow. Nor will we be receiving you, Barlow. Not at my country estate. Not in town. Nowhere."

Wendel shook his head, his expression a mixture of anger and sorrow. "We'll see." He opened the door and stepped out.

Arthur sucked in a deep breath. He forced his fists to unclench, then raised a shaking hand to rub his forehead.

"Are you well, sir?" Charles asked.

Arthur shook his head. "I am not."

"Should I send for anyone, sir?"

"No." Wendel had made one good point. Miss Christine's reputation would be more or less restored if she married. That would solve at least one of the day's troubles. "I'll be in my office. I have a letter to write. I am not to be disturbed." He turned to look his butler in the eye. "And Charles? Make sure my sister doesn't leave the premises."

"Very well, sir."

Chapter Twenty-Two

Daphne sat in the parlor window watching carriages rumble past their townhome. She could, now. Not like in the days directly following the publication of Christine's letter. Then, every passing carriage held gawkers, gaping out their windows and pointing. Anytime they spotted Daphne peeking around the parlor curtain, their expressions would curl with scorn. Fortunately, as December wound down, thoughts turned to the Yuletide Season. Now, everyone without seemed either harried or cheerful and made no attempt to peer within.

Which meant that Daphne could at least watch the world, even if she could not go out in it. All their invitations had been rescinded. No callers came. Mr. Garrick and his sister had left for the country in an abrupt fashion, likely so they would not be forced to choose between Daphne's family and the remainder of society. She and her family existed within the bubble of their townhome while Father concluded what business he meant to conduct in London and Mother planned their imminent departure.

Daphne let out a sigh. If only… If only many things. Christine hadn't written that letter, or at least hadn't entrusted it to Wendy. Or, if only Mr. Garrick had kissed Daphne, or she'd parted with him in less anger. For certainly, now he would remember her that way, sharp and bitter. Like as not, she would never see him again. She swallowed down the lump that rose in her throat at that oft-repeated thought and tried to focus on the passersby.

A familiar carriage turned onto the street. Daphne's eyes flew wide. He must mean to call on them. His carriage on their street in London was too much of a coincidence otherwise. Daphne surged to her feet and ran to find her sister. Mr. Ryan Quincy was about to arrive.

She flung open the door to Christine's room to find her sister sprawled atop her coverlet in a disastrous state; hair disheveled and gown wrinkled, her fair skin marred by a dark ring under each eye.

"Hurry, get up. You must make ready."

Christine turned her head and gazed dully at Daphne for a moment before returning to contemplation of her ceiling.

Daphne crossed the room and grabbed her sister's arm to tug. "Mr. Quincy's carriage is coming down the street. You must get up. Don a different gown. Let me brush your hair."

"Ryan is here?" Christine sprang from the bed and pushed past Daphne to run from the room.

Daphne stumbled back, arms cartwheeling as she regained her balance. She stood for a moment, stunned, then whirled to follow her sister. The moment she stepped into the hall, she heard her father's voice. It grew in volume and clarity as she rushed to the top of the staircase.

"...arrive on our doorstep, Mr. Quincy." Father's tone held frost.

"Please, Father," Christine begged.

Daphne rounded the corner to find her sister halfway down the stairs, blocked by their father and Edward standing shoulder to shoulder at the base. Mr. Quincy stood in the entrance hall, hat and gloves clutched in his hands.

Father angled a look over his shoulder at Christine. "You know my decision. You may not wed this man until his debts are paid."

"But Father, please. I love him." Christine's words were garbled by tears, but intelligible enough.

Mr. Quincy, expression strained, took a step forward. "I am aware of your stipulation, sir, which is why I have stayed away, but you should know that I was summoned to London and informed that all my debts are paid."

Christine gasped, hands flying to her mouth.

Daphne descended to wrap an arm about her sister, worried she might faint on the staircase.

Mr. Quincy tugged a page from his coat pocket and proffered it to their father. "Here."

Both topped with wavy brown hair, her father's and Edward's heads bent near as they studied the page.

Father turned it over, then back, then over again. Finally, he offered it back to Mr. Quincy. "That seems in order."

"I assure you, Mr. Hayhurst, it is. I would never

court your daughter under false pretenses."

Father nodded.

Daphne squeezed Christine tight. Beneath Daphne's arm, her sister trembled.

"But how?" Edward said.

Mr. Quincy shook his head. "I was not informed of who paid the debts. It was done anonymously."

"Did you do it, Father?" Christine gasped.

At the base of the steps, their father turned to look up at her. "I cannot take credit."

"What is transpiring?"

Daphne craned her neck to see her mother at the top of the staircase.

Christine pulled free of Daphne's grip and raced up the steps to their mother. "Someone has paid Mr. Quincy's debts. We're free to marry now." She swiveled back, one arm snaking out to grab the railing as she swayed. "We can marry now, can't we, Father?"

He frowned. "I would like to know the identity of this mysterious benefactor first."

"Paul," Mother said sharply. She turned a smile on Christine. "You and Mr. Quincy may certainly marry now, dear."

With a squeal of delight, Christine flung her arms about their mother.

"But first, you must come with me," Mother said. "You are a sight, dear. Let the gentlemen speak on the details while we get your hair and gown put right."

Christine made no protest as their mother led her away. She did look back, though, her radiant smile making her beautiful despite her rumpled state. The smile Mr. Quincy returned matched Christine's perfectly.

"You really have no idea who paid your debts?" Edward said.

Mr. Quincy turned to him. "I rather assumed your father had."

Father shook his head. "I assure you, I did not." He glanced back up the staircase, his gaze traveling past Daphne. "Perhaps I should have."

"Maybe the Barlows did, to make amends for what Cousin Wendy did?" Daphne suggested. She could imagine her aunt and Wendel being so kind.

"I did get a glimpse of the signature on the documents," Mr. Quincy said. "They shuffled the page away too quickly for me to read the name, but I think the initials were A and G."

A jolt shot through Daphne. Edward looked up to meet her gaze and cocked an eyebrow. With no true justification for her certainty, Daphne shook her head. She couldn't assure her brother it was Mr. Garrick. There was no true way to know that, except that her heart felt it to be so.

"Daphne," her mother's voice called from the upper hall.

"Go and help your mother and sister," her father ordered. "Mr. Quincy and I have much to discuss."

Daphne nodded and retreated up the steps as the gentlemen went deeper into the house, likely to her father's study.

She and her mother, with the help of two maids, did their best to make Christine presentable. They bathed her face in rose water, had her change into a freshly pressed gown, and brushed and curled her hair. Mother sent for her face paints, but Christine would have none of that, too eager to return to Mr. Quincy. Finally, resigned, their mother agreed, and Christine rushed away. Daphne and her mother followed at a more decorous pace. The gentlemen awaited them in the front parlor, standing when they entered.

Christine rushed to Mr. Quincy and took his hands in hers. "It is settled, then?"

"It is. A license has been requested, your father's gift to us. We will be husband and wife before the Yuletide."

Christine let out a squeal of delight and threw her arms about him. Mr. Quincy returned the embrace, eyes closing and expression wreathed in contentment. Daphne's father cleared his throat. Slowly, as if to do so pained him, Mr. Quincy set Christine away, though he still kept one of her hands clasped in his.

A sickening pit of pain opened in Daphne's gut. She recalled Mr. Garrick's words, that he knew he hadn't loved Wendy because she had never enticed him to throw propriety away. Daphne blinked back tears. Would any man ever love her enough to forget himself and embrace her right in front of her relations?

If she ever received the opportunity again, no matter who watched, she would kiss Arthur.

"Yes, well, well wishes are in order," Edward said. "I must admit, I'm rather relieved that I don't have to fight you, Quincy."

"Fight him?" Christine gasped.

"For your honor and all that."

Christine angled her chin into the air. "I would never have permitted you to."

"You wouldn't be able to stop me. It's a gentlemen's affair. Nothing to do with you."

"You, moments ago, said it would be over my honor."

A glance showed that their mother appeared, for once, pleased to hear her children argue. Daphne forced a hollow smile, wishing their banter could induce joy in her as well.

"Should we sit?" Mother said. "I'll send for tea."

"Not only tea, I hope," Edward said. "A celebration calls for something stronger."

"Excuse me sirs, madams, but Mr. Garrick wishes to know if Mr. Edward is at home."

They all turned to find their butler in the doorway.

Daphne's heart leaped into her throat. "Edward?" she repeated before she could halt the word. Not her? Mr. Garrick had returned to London, but not for her?

"Show him in," Edward said. "He can share in the good news."

The butler retreated but no one sat. In moments, new footfalls sounded, coming their way.

Mr. Garrick appeared in the parlor doorway, then rocked back on his heels slightly as he took in the room. He gave a general nod and turned to

Edward. "Hayhurst, have you seen Wendel Barlow about?"

"Mr. Garrick, do come in and join us for tea," Mother said.

"I beg your pardon, Mrs. Hayhurst, Mr. Hayhurst, but I am in an extreme hurry. I must borrow your son."

His gaze met Daphne's and she read the strain in his eyes before he turned once more to Edward. "Hayhurst?"

Christine stepped forward, dragging Mr. Quincy with her. "Mr. Garrick, I do not mean to be unpleasant, but we're in the middle of a celebration. Mr. Quincy and I are to be wed."

Mr. Garrick turned to Christine and bowed. The movement lacked his usual grace, each motion stiff. "Felicitations. I do not mean to infringe, Miss Christine, and I am pleased to see you well, but I require your brother."

"Can it not wait?"

The frown Edward turned on Christine mimicked Daphne's feeling. "Give over, Christine. It's obviously important."

"You can't know that. He hasn't said why he wishes to find our cousin. It might be a matter of a gambling debt or a wager. We have no way to know it's important."

"Garrick wouldn't barge in like this if it weren't."

Mr. Garrick scrubbed long fingers across his forehead.

"I'm certain our celebration can wait a

moment," Mr. Quincy said.

"We've already waited for years."

Daphne's parents exchanged a pained look.

Mother stepped up beside Christine. "Come now, dear, let's go and see about tea and something stronger for the gentlemen."

"But I don't wish to leave Ryan's side. Not ever again."

"If I could have a moment, Hayhurst," Mr. Garrick said, causing both Edward and Daphne's father to turn to him.

Christine issued another protest, Mother and Mr. Quincy working to calm her. Edward made to cross the room to Mr. Garrick, but Christine stepped into his way, pulling Mr. Quincy off balance and into a small table. The vase atop tumbled to crash on the floor. Mother cried out and a curse issued from Daphne's father. Mr. Garrick frowned and pivoted away.

"Enough," Daphne snapped, loud enough to be heard over the babble. "I realize we have all been under strain, but this is ridiculous. Franklin, Irving, Justina and Katherine are not even here, yet our home sounds as if inhabited by a gaggle of children. Mr. Garrick, who unequivocally offered this family assistance when we were sunk in scandal, arrived here in distress and with the very simple request of speaking with Edward. We will afford him that." She strode to her brother's side and took his arm. "Send for tea and for a maid to sweep up the vase. Edward and I will return shortly."

Ignoring the stunned faces about the room, Daphne tugged Edward along as she marched them to the parlor doorway, where Mr. Garrick stood, facing them again. Reaching him, she wrapped her free hand about his bicep and dragged him along as well, trying not to notice that her slender fingers didn't even reach halfway around. She marched the two men down the hall to a much smaller parlor and inside. Releasing them, she closed the door.

"Thank you," Mr. Garrick said, making no move to sit.

"So, what's the trouble?" Edward asked.

Mr. Garrick reached into his coat and pulled out a folded paper. "It's my sister. She..." He swallowed. "She's run off. With Barlow."

Daphne couldn't stifle a gasp.

Edward took the page and unfolded it. "'Since you refuse to see reason,'" he read, "'I am forced to take matters into my own hands.'" He looked up with a frown. "What does she mean?"

"That's who she's in love with," Daphne breathed.

"Barlow?" Edward scowled. "She chose him over me?"

Mr. Garrick nodded.

"Well I'll be damned," Edward muttered.

"What does she mean when she says you won't see reason?" Daphne asked.

Mr. Garrick scrubbed a hand over his face, which did nothing to ease the lines of worry there. "He came to me and told me he loves her. They said they wished to wed, but I kicked him out and removed her from London. I thought that some time in the country, away from him, would restore reason to her."

"But she ran off," Daphne concluded when Mr. Garrick fell silent.

"Where to?" Edward asked.

"I've no idea. I hoped, being in town still, you might have heard something?"

Daphne shook her head. "We haven't been out. What with the scandal, no one would see us."

"We would have heard something," Edward said. "If they were in London, we would know."

"If they're truly in love, they would have gone north, to Scotland," Daphne said. "At least, we may hope so."

She shuddered to think of the scandal, otherwise. Miss Garrick would be ruined if they hadn't gone north to wed. Daphne suppressed a sigh. Both Christine and Miss Garrick inspired such devotion. Though Daphne didn't wish for a scandal, she couldn't help but envy the younger women for the dedication they inspired.

"That's it, then," Edward said. "We'll have to go north and find them. If they aren't married, I'll see Wendel propose or he'll meet me on the field of honor."

"We?" Mr. Garrick said, a note of relief in his tone.

"Aye. He's my cousin. He hasn't a father. It's my duty to see he does right by your sister."

"Thank you."

"I'll have my horse saddled and a few things

packed." Edward departed the room, the door left wide open behind him.

"It's good of your brother to help," Mr. Garrick said softly.

"I only wish that I could as well." How she longed to smooth the lines of pain and worry from his brow.

"You can best help by staying safe and well with your family." He bowed. "And I thank you for your assistance today."

Daphne nodded, wishing desperately that she had reassurance to give.

"Please ask your brother to meet me at my townhome. I will pack some few items as well. I believe he does not mean for us to be slowed down by a carriage, and I approve."

"I will tell him."

Mr. Garrick nodded, then walked past her out of the parlor door. If she reached out a hand, she could grab his arm again. Pull him back.

Instead, she let him pass.

"Mr. Garrick?" His name sprang to her lips unbidden.

He swiveled to face her, expression quizzical. "Yes?"

Give me some sign of your affection. "Good luck."

"Thank you, Miss Hayhurst." He bowed again and strode away down the hall.

Chapter Twenty-Three

"Mr. Hayhurst," Charles announced.

At that announcement by his butler, Arthur halted from pacing his library and swiveled to face the door. He glanced at the mantle clock. Only a quarter of an hour had passed since Arthur had arrived at his townhome. Hayhurst was quick. Stenson, who insisted on riding with them, hadn't even finished packing their bags.

Hayhurst strode in, dressed for riding, and offered a nod of greeting. "Ready, Garrick?"

"Nearly so."

"Before I left, I asked Christine if she knows anything." He held up a hand to ward off Arthur's protest. "I know, you assumed I knew that your sister's circumstance should remain quiet. I do. I tried to play it off as interest on my part. Christine is too astute, though. Most likely because you showed up at our door asking for our cousin. Regardless, she said she doesn't know with whom your sister is in love, but she does know that Miss Garrick's love is real and that we ought not to interfere. She's quite certain your sister will have gone north to marry."

Arthur nodded and crossed to the various maps he'd laid out on the table. "Assuming he came for her, which the carriage tracks I found suggest, they left from our country home, here."

"If you found tracks, why not follow them?" Hayhurst crossed to Arthur's side to peer down at the map.

Arthur pointed to a tee in the road. "They joined this roadway running north and south, which is very busy this time of year, and the tracks became obscured. They appeared to turn south at first, but it was difficult to say. That slight chance, and the hope that you had seen your cousin, brought me here."

"Even if they turned south at the tee, there's no way to know it wasn't a ruse."

Arthur nodded, having considered the same thing. "Assuming your sisters are correct that marriage is their goal, they should have gone due north there."

"They'd want to wed quickly," Hayhurst said. "Before we caught them."

"They've likely succeeded in that," Arthur muttered.

Hayhurst tapped the map. "They'll have gone here. It's the nearest town across the border."

A knock on the doorframe brought Arthur around to find Stenson. "Sir, all is ready."

Arthur nodded. "Hayhurst, meet my valet, Stenson. He's accompanying us. Stenson, Edward Hayhurst."

"Valet?" Hayhurst repeated. "I'd the impression we're in a hurry, Garrick."

"We are. Stenson is an excellent horseman."

"I will not impede you, Mr. Hayhurst."

Hayhurst shrugged. "Whatever you say,

Garrick. I'm only along in case Cousin Wendel requires assistance to do what's right by your sister."

"Right. Shall we, then?" Arthur led the way out the door.

Riding fast, they left London as quickly as the congested streets allowed. Once free of the city, Arthur nudged his mount into a canter, alternating that pace with walking. When their mounts flagged, they paid men to return them to the city and hired new beasts. They broke only to eat and collapse into bed in the evenings, but it still took days to reach the town where they felt his sister and Barlow must have gone.

To Arthur's relief, they learned that his sister and Barlow had arrived and been wed immediately. To his chagrin, they'd already departed. By all reports, they hadn't returned to England, instead heading deeper into Scotland. Arthur sent Stenson back with the news and orders for his staff, and to see if his sister had made any effort to get a message back to England.

He and Hayhurst kept on their trail.

Days later found them still in Scotland, following a steeply winding road to a small village on the coast. Deep in Arthur's gut, fear that Barlow and Lillian had taken a ship soured. He chafed his hands together in the December cold and urged his mount faster, to no avail. Their stocky Highland mounts would not be hurried, but what they lacked in speed they made up for in surefootedness and endurance.

Hayhurst looked over from where he rode alongside Arthur. "If we don't find them soon, we'll miss the Yuletide and be forced to endure Hogmanay instead."

"You've already missed much of the celebration and your sister's wedding," Arthur said, for word of the date on which Miss Christine would wed had caught up with them a few short days ago. "If we don't find them in this town you should head back. You have a family with whom to celebrate the season."

"What about you?"

Arthur shrugged. "I'll keep looking. With my uncle gone, Lillian is my only family."

"Not so. You have a new brother."

Arthur offered a rusty chuckle. "I always thought Barlow would end up my brother. I simply saw it happening a different way."

"Aye. I always thought the same about Quincy."

"You thought he would marry a different sister?" Arthur said, strain touching his voice.

"No. I thought he'd marry Christine, but without a scandal."

Arthur nodded and turned his attention back up the roadway.

"You could easily have more family." Hayhurst's tone was tentative.

"What do you mean?" Arthur asked sharply.

Had Miss Christine told Hayhurst more about Lillian than he'd admitted? Did she and Barlow continue to run because she was with child? Arthur would throttle Wendel Barlow to within an inch of his life, new brother or no.

"I mean, Daphne fancies you."

Arthur's head snapped around. He stared at Hayhurst. "What makes you say that?"

"Come, man. Anyone can see as much in the way she looks at you, and I've never seen her stand up to our family before. Not once. She yelled at the lot of us, even Mother and Father. She did that for you."

Arthur shook his head. He more than fancied her. He knew she… held him in some esteem, but enough? He had no intention of having his heart crushed again in such rapid succession, by cousins, no less. Aside from which, Daphne had admitted fear that his love for her was fleeting.

"What's stopping you?" Hayhurst asked as they crested a rise to find a picturesque Scottish village tucked into the valley below.

"Your sister expressed a lack of certainty in the robustness of my affection."

Hayhurst snorted. "Ridiculous. You two look at each other exactly the same way Christine and Quincy do. If that's what's worrying her, simply prove her wrong."

Arthur shrugged. His mount started down the hill, surefooted despite the slope. "I have made an effort. It does not seem to be enough, and I have no intention of tendering an offer that will not be accepted."

"Ah."

They plodded down the slope in silence, the dwellings below growing ever larger. Finally,

Arthur could restrain the words no more and asked, "What does 'ah' mean?"

"Only that, I know how downright terrified I was to ask for your sister's hand. I understand. You're afraid."

Arthur ground his teeth together. What did Hayhurst know? He hadn't even loved Lillian. Not truly. He'd never imagined a life with a woman for years only to have her crush his dreams beneath her slippered foot and grind them into the carpet. He didn't know true pain.

"I am not afraid."

"Of course you are. You're afraid she'll say no, like Cousin Wendy did." Hayhurst glanced his way. "Not really fair, that. Punishing Daphne for what Wendy has done. Sort of like punishing Wendel for what she's done. I mean, I wager before she turned you down, you would have been happy to see Wendel marry your sister. I understand, though. Wendy got in your head and messed about in there."

Arthur's jaws clenched so hard, pain shot up to his temples.

"Hey, that's Wendel's carriage," Hayhurst exclaimed.

Arthur followed Hayhurst's pointing finger to what looked to be the town's only inn, and that not very large. Without stood a familiar carriage. Arthur's gaze narrowed, his anger finding a new focus.

They rode down into the town and straight to the inn. Arthur jumped from the saddle, not caring what happened to his hired mount. Vaguely, he noted Hayhurst tossing a few coins to the kilted men who came forward to collect the beasts. Arthur took the inn steps two at a time and burst through the door.

An elderly gentleman looked up from behind a counter and said something in Scottish.

Not caring what the man might mean, Arthur said in English, "I'm looking for my sister and her… husband. She has black hair like mine and gray eyes. She—"

"Arthur," Lillian's voice cried, full of joy.

He turned left, to the common room, and found her rushing up to him. She flung her arms about his neck and squeezed. Seen over her shoulder, Wendel came to his feet at a table. He moved around behind his chair, hands resting on the back, his expression uncertain.

Lillian pulled back. "I knew you would come to bring us home for Christmas. Wendel insisted that we keep moving because he said if you found us too soon, you would have the marriage annulled, which I said was impossible, but he's very afraid you're angry, but it's nearly Christmas and I missed you."

Arthur closed his eyes and hugged his sister close. Much of his anger drained away. "I missed you as well."

Lillian pulled back again and looked up. "So we can come home for Christmas and you won't challenge Wendel? I truly do love him, you know. I won't let you hurt him."

Arthur looked over her head at Wendel again, who still regarded them with a worried expression. The inn door swung open.

"Miss Garrick," Hayhurst exclaimed. "That is, rather, Mrs. Barlow."

Lillian turned to Hayhurst with a tentative smile. "What about, 'Cousin Lillian?'"

Hayhurst gave a decisive nod. "'Cousin Lillian' it is." He started to turn. "Where is… ah, Barlow, there you are," he finished, voice deepening with menace. He took a step in Wendel's direction.

Arthur caught Hayhurst by the shoulder. "Leave it."

Hayhurst turned back, surprised. "Leave it? After the trouble he's caused?"

Lillian stepped around Hayhurst. "You mean, I caused. Everything has been my idea." She glanced at Wendel. When she turned back, she wore a fond smile. "If you must know, he put up quite the fight. He said it would be wrong to woo me." She rolled her eyes heavenward. "Isn't that silly? How wrong can it be to be so happy?" She narrowed her gaze past Hayhurst to Arthur. "And before you answer, know that I believe our happiness to be worth defying you, even if you are my family."

A jolt shot through Arthur, having nothing to do with the defection of both sister and closest friend. Daphne had rebuked her family for him and he'd all but ignored her show of solidarity. Was he, as Hayhurst claimed, punishing her for what Wendy had done? Was he afraid?

"Come, dearest." Lillian held out a hand to

Wendel.

He immediately started forward. When he reached them, Lillian took his hand. They turned to face Arthur and Hayhurst together. Suddenly, Arthur became aware of a myriad of curious faces, from patrons in the taproom to other diners, to the inn staff.

"So, you, ah, haven't come here to kill me?" Wendel asked.

Hayhurst turned a questioning look on Arthur. Lillian leveled a glare at them both. Ever so faintly, Arthur could see the lingering discoloration on Wendel's jaw, where his fist had connected. "You and my sister are wed? You have papers to prove that?"

Wendel nodded. He patted his coat pocket. "Most certainly. There were witnesses as well. Many. I made certain."

"And nothing… untoward happened before the ceremony took place?"

Lillian gasped. "Arthur."

He ignored her, locking eyes with Wendel, who shook his head. Arthur let out a sigh and rubbed his forehead. "Well then, there is little left but to offer my well wishes."

Lillian let out a cry of delight and hugged him again. Arthur hugged her back, sorrow washing through him. Now he would be well and truly alone.

"Thank you," Wendel said when she stepped back. He proffered his hand.

Arthur shook and forced the correct words past

the pain in his chest. "Congratulations, Brother."

Hayhurst repeated the gesture, though he sounded a touch put out in his well wishes too. Then his expression brightened. "Well then, since neither of us plans to challenge Cousin Wendel, let's say we all head to my father's country seat? He throws a fabulous ball every Yuletide. You'll love it."

"Oh, can we?" Lillian said. "That would be lovely."

Arthur shrugged, unable to shake his sorrow quite enough to care. "If you like."

"Will, ah, Wendy be there?" Wendel asked.

Arthur certainly hoped not.

Lillian turned to Wendel. "Do you care?"

Wendel's expression firmed. "No. No I don't."

Hayhurst let out an explosive breath. "That's a relief because I believe she's been banned, but Aunt Barlow was invited. We've been out of touch, so I haven't heard if she accepted." He gestured to the door. "I realize that it's a bit late, but we'd best get a move on. By carriage, we'll barely make it."

Their course decided, Wendel crossed to the innkeeper to settle up while Hayhurst went to see about fresh mounts and the coachman for Wendel's carriage. Lillian crossed to a woman Arthur assumed to be the innkeeper's wife to attempt to convey their need for food to eat on their journey. Arthur remained standing in the inn's entryway, feeling quite alone.

Lillian and Wendel both finished their errands. With eyes only for each other, they crossed back to meet near Arthur. His sister held out a hand to Wendel, who gazed at her with a look so tender, Arthur had to avert his eyes. He tried to tamp down jealousy, but it gurgled up from within regardless.

He wanted what his sister and Wendel had. He loved someone that much. He should be willing to do whatever it took to be with her, as Lillian and Wendel had. What had Hayhurst advised? If Daphne doubted Arthur, he must simply prove his love to her.

Chapter Twenty-Four

Unnoticed by those below, Daphne peeked between the spindles of the banister, through the entrance hall and into the ballroom. Just as when she'd been a child, she knelt on the floor. Unlike then, a puddle of gauzy sage muslin and delicately beaded lace encircled her. Also unlike then, Daphne felt not a hint of joy or anticipation. Mostly, she simply wished to sit unnoticed, an inelegant puddle on the floor.

She closed her eyes and took in the bright scent of pine boughs. They decorated the home from end to end, top to bottom. Even the servants' quarters, though those mostly lacked the addition of frosted pinecones, bright ribbons, and red-berried holly. The servants' quarters did, however, boast a lace, ribbon, and nut decorated kissing bough, as did the arched entrance to the ballroom.

As she watched, Edward lured all three of Mr. Quincy's sisters, aged from fifteen to his own nineteen years, under the arch from which hung the bough. He kissed the hand of each of the younger two, then, when the eldest extended her glove-clad fingers, he stepped forward and touched his lips to hers. All three squealed in delight and ran off. Daphne shook her head. Were it not Christmas, her brother would pay for his impertinence with a betrothal.

Which would likely make yet another happy couple. Daphne let out a sigh and closed her eyes to blot out the festivities, but that didn't fend off visions of what transpired.

Her younger brothers, dressed as gentlemen, did their duty dancing with the local girls their age. Her youngest two sisters, older already than Daphne when she'd spied through the railing as a child, ran about below, slowing only when they realized an adult scrutinized them.

Her new cousin, Lillian, danced, yet again, with Wendel. Though it was ill form for them to dance almost exclusively with one another, everyone's expressions turned to doting tolerance when aimed their way. Daphne imagined the same latitude would be extended to Christine and Mr. Quincy but they, cheerful and smiling the whole time, alternated dancing together with partnering anyone who would stand up with them.

Out of all the couples below, Daphne's own parents graced the dance floor the least. Far less, in truth, than usual, but no rift existed there. Daphne's mother was simply preoccupied with entertaining Aunt Barlow and with showing her about the house. More often than Daphne had ever heard before, her mother's laughter bubbled forth and any glimpse caught of her revealed a smile.

Their friends and neighbors, their relations, everyone in Daphne's world, gathered below. They were all happy. The manor house glowed with candlelight. Chandeliers and sconces dripped crystal. The fresh scent of pinesap layered with cinnamon and apple. Music filled the ballroom, spilled into the entrance hall, and wafted up to tantalize her ears… and she could not muster care, for Mr. Garrick had not come.

When Edward, Lillian and Wendel had arrived on Christmas Eve, they'd assured her Mr. Garrick was on his way. He'd ridden out ahead of them, making better time than they could in Wendel's carriage. They'd expected him to beat them. Instead, all that had arrived was a note saying that he would arrive shortly. Daphne had stayed up late into the night, watching the yule log burn, but he'd never appeared.

Something warm splattered onto her hand, felt through the thin material of her glove. She looked down to a droplet soaking into the fabric, followed by another, and another. It took her a moment to realize they were her tears. She swiped hands across her cheeks, turning the material gray with moisture.

That was that, then. She couldn't go down with gloves that appeared smudged with dirt. She stripped them off. She would have to slink back to her room and dry them by the fire. If they were presentable in time, maybe she would find the will to descend before the party ended. Gloves in one hand, she grasped the railing with the other and pulled, coming to her feet.

A knock sounded below. Daphne's heart stuttered. Their butler stepped forward to open the door. A tall form strode through in a swirl of wind that set the candle flames in the entrance hall into jumbled motion. He doffed his hat, revealing wavy black hair, and peeled off his gloves, then removed his greatcoat, handing each to their butler in turn. Daphne stared down at him with her heart lodged in her throat, hardly able to breathe, let alone speak.

"I've come to see Miss Hayhurst."

"Do you not mean, sir, that you have come for the Hayhurst's ball?" the butler asked.

Mr. Garrick shook his head. "Indeed not. I mean precisely what I said. I have come for Miss Hayhurst."

Daphne opened her mouth to call out to him, but her throat was too tight for words. His face lifted, gaze seeking. His eyes locked with hers. Ignoring the sputtered protest of their butler, he crossed to the staircase.

Barely able to breathe past her throbbing heart, Daphne rushed to the top of the staircase and hurried down. On the last step, she stopped, suddenly aware that she did not know Mr. Garrick's intention. What she did know was that anyone looking through the arched ballroom doorway could see them. She wouldn't trap him into a union by doing something so wayward as flinging her arms about him… as she so wished to do.

"Mr. Garrick," she managed, his name a whisper on her lips.

He bowed. "Miss Hayhurst."

"You've finally arrived."

"You have been waiting for me?"

"I worried you wouldn't come."

He patted his coat pocket, where something crinkled. "I had to go first to get a license."

Did he mean, so they might wed? "A license?"

He held out a hand. "Yes. Your sister had one so I thought you should as well, though the archbishop is beginning to wonder at the sanity of Hayhurst women."

Daphne settled her hand into his before realizing she'd dropped her gloves somewhere in her rush to greet him. Their skin met in a surge of warmth that spread up her arm to suffuse her being. Deep within, something eased. A wrongness put right by his touch. Hand in his, she descended the final step.

He looked about, gaze settling on the kissing bough hung in the arched doorway to the ballroom. With a gentle tug, he led her across the entrance hall.

"What are you doing?" she asked, breathless. "People are starting to look."

"Not enough. I wish everyone to witness my esteem for you. Could I, I would say what I have come to say before the whole of the known world."

Daphne let out a gasp. He must mean to propose. What else could he plan? "You… you mean to ask me to be your wife? Here? Now?"

He paused, turning to her. Inside the ballroom, more and more of their guests halted their chatter and steps to watch through the doorway. Her hand still clasped in his, he raised the other to stroke her cheek. Recalling how she'd botched things when last they met, Daphne worked to suppress a shudder of delight.

"Are the special license and public proposal not a grand enough gesture?" Mr. Garrick asked softly. "You asked me to prove that my love for you is such that I'm willing to throw off propriety. Requesting your hand before all these people, when I haven't even sought your father's permission, is the only means I can imagine by which to do so without disrespecting you. I will flout the mores of society to prove my love, but I will never prove it by compromising your virtue."

Daphne gazed into his stormy gray eyes. Her hand trembled in his. She drew in a shaky breath, too afraid to shatter such a perfect moment to voice her reply.

"Daphne?" he asked in that same quiet, hopeful tone.

She didn't need words. Instead, she squeezed his hand tighter and pulled him the remainder of the distance to the archway. She halted them beneath the kissing bough and turned to face him. Inside the ballroom, a murmur rose. Though the musicians played on, Daphne doubted a single couple still danced. She felt hundreds of eyes upon them.

"I love you, Arthur." Rising to her tiptoes beneath the Yuletide bough, she pulled his head down and kissed him.

Gasps sounded, quickly drowned out by applause. He wrapped her in his arms and lifted her from her feet, deepening their kiss. She twined her arms about his neck. He'd finally declared his love. Her heart was so full, she knew he would never let her go.

But he did. Expression reluctant, he set her on her feet, then smoothed back curls that had somehow come loose during their embrace. Capturing her hand again, he dropped to one knee. Vaguely, Daphne heard more gasps, tinged with joy rather than startlement, though little sound penetrated the pounding of her pulse in her ears.

"Daphne Hayhurst," Arthur said, gray eyes showing no hint of a storm. "You bring light and joy into my world. I refuse to endure another moment without you. To put it simply, I love you. Please, will you be my wife?"

Daphne tried to swallow back the lump of joy clogging her throat. She couldn't say the wrong thing now, could she?

She drew in a deep breath. "Yes."

He sprang to his feet. To her joy, she was in his arms again. As she kissed Arthur Garrick soundly before the whole of society, Daphne knew that his love was the most wonderful Yuletide gift ever.

Arthur let the book he read rest open on the arm of his chair, watching Daphne rather than taking in the words on the page. His wife particularly enjoyed letters from her family. Bathed in a mixture of firelight and candlelight, her shimmering locks glinting with gold and red, she perused the page. He traced her features with his gaze, sure he'd never seen anything so lovely as Daphne curled in a chair in their favorite parlor.

She looked up with a frown. "Christine still maintains she will not attend Mother and Father's Yuletide ball if Wendy is invited."

Arthur shrugged. "Do you blame her?"

"It's been five years. Cousin Wendy has become very contrite."

"She isn't contrite. She's desperate. Six and twenty and still unwed, she's willing to humble herself to capitalize on your family's connections."

Daphne's frown deepened. "Has Lillian said aught? Do she and Wendel believe Wendy should be forgiven?"

"Certainly. Wendel has ever been quick to forgive his sister, and Lillian is kind-hearted." Arthur offered a smile. "Like you."

He forwent pointing out that Wendel would be forever responsible for Wendy should she not secure a husband, something he undoubtedly wished to avoid.

"You have not forgiven her, then?"

Arthur shook his head. "I have. That doesn't mean I wish to spend the Yuletide with her." His gaze settled on Daphne's lips. "Why endure her during my favorite time of year?"

The pink bow of Daphne's mouth turned up at the corners. "You realize that we scandalize everyone anew, yearly, when you kiss me under the kissing bough. Last year, I believe someone suggested dousing us with punch to cool our ardor."

"As I recall, you're the one who wound her fingers into my hair and wouldn't let go."

"I daresay you didn't wish me to."

Arthur chuckled, unable to refute that. "True enough. You see how wonderful the Yuletide is? Why spoil that by including Miss Barlow?"

Daphne's frown reappeared. "Your dislike is more understandable. Her treatment of Christine, while vile, resulted in my sister getting what she wished for most, whereas you lost a considerable sum."

"I have no notion to what you refer." Arthur raised his book in pretend interest but didn't keep his amusement from his face. Daphne often attempted to trap him into an admission.

Though his relations were very nearly positive he was Mr. Quincy's anonymous benefactor, Arthur would never admit as much. To do so would put Quincy in the awkward position of being able to pay him back. Quincy did an admirable job managing his small estate and had invested his wife's dowry well, but he could ill afford to repay Arthur. If Quincy had paid the debts himself, he'd likely still have three years to go before meeting Mr. Hayhurst's requirement to marry his daughter. Instead, the two seemed blissfully happy and had provided Arthur and Daphne's daughter and son with two cousins.

That thought brought a fresh smile. One of Arthur's favorite aspects of the Hayhursts' annual celebration was the gathering of children. Having lived the first twenty-odd years of his life with a very small family, Arthur enjoyed watching his daughter and son run about with the Quincys' two girls and Lillian and Wendel's twins. Yuletide, with the decorations, food, relations, and friends, truly had become his favorite celebration.

"Arthur," Daphne called.

He looked over the book to meet her lovely amber eyes. "Yes, dear?"

"I love you, even if you do keep this one secret from me."

"That is very kind of you." He went back to pretending to read.

"Arthur," Daphne repeated his name in mock indignation.

"Yes, dear?"

"Aren't you forgetting something?"

Arthur closed the book, setting it aside as he stood. He crossed the room to her and extended his hand. She placed her palm in his.

"I love you, too," he said and pulled her into a

kiss that proved it. As much as Arthur enjoyed the Yuletide, he reserved the right to pretend they stood under a kissing bough whenever they wished, no matter what the season.

~ THE END ~

Join Summer Hanford's email list and get free
stuff!

Sign up for free books, sneak previews, new
release alerts, news, giveaways and more!

Visit: **https://geni.us/RomanceMailSignUp**

Enjoy Summer's work? Please consider leaving a review. Reviews are a source of inspiration for authors and a great help with sales, both because of the information they provide potential readers and because they let amazon know you care.

To leave a review today, go to:
https://getbook.at/HisYuletideKiss

Thank you!

ABOUT the AUTHOR

Summer Hanford

Summer Hanford is an author of sweet, adventure filled Historical Romance, *Pride and Prejudice* retellings, and High Fantasy, and writes her Romance Novels under L Summer Hanford. She lives in New York with her husband and compulsory, deliberately spoiled, cats. The newest addition to their household, an energetic setter-shepherd mix, is (still) not yet appreciated by any of the cats but is well loved by the humans.

For more about Summer, visit:
www.summerhanford.com

www.ingramcontent.com/pod-product-compliance
Lightning Source LLC
Chambersburg PA
CBHW021128190726
48288CB00008B/2551